James Skipworth and the Catfish Colonel

A Farce in Two Acts

by Cy Young

A SAMUEL FRENCH ACTING EDITION

FOUNDED 1830

New York Hollywood London Toronto

SAMUELFRENCH.COM

SYNOPSIS OF SCENES

Time: The Present

ACT I

Helen Osborne's Office on New York's
chic east side

ACT II

The Same

The set should be light and airy. This is a comedy and
needs to be brightly lit. The set pieces should look modern and simple (not heavy). There will be frenzied activity
on stage and the performers should not have to compete
with the set for the audience's attention.

JAMES SKIPWORTH
AND
THE CATFISH COLONEL

ACT I

SCENE: The set is the snappy east side office of producer/actress HELEN OSBORNE, an attractive, 40-year-old woman. The set reflects Helen's feminine good taste and New York sophistication. Right Center is a desk, behind it a leather chair on casters. The desk is cluttered: contracts and theatrical photographs are stacked beside a huge pile of unopened manilla envelopes containing play manuscripts, and a phone with a long extension cord (20 feet) sits next to a Tony statue. On the back wall, Far Right, is a small, closed window through which buildings can be seen. On the floor beneath the window is an umbrella stand with an umbrella peeking out. Left of the window and behind the desk is the bathroom, the door of which opens inward and toward Center Stage. There is a couch Up Center on which are arranged a number of brightly colored pillows. Left of the couch on the wall are some photographs of a sexy woman in a bathing suit. The door to the outside hall is Up Left with the door opening inward and Upstage. It has an opaque glass transom at the top which is operated by a rod Stage Left of the

door. Below the door is a bookcase on the wall Left contain-
ing a number of paperback plays and a hardcover edition of
Shakespeare's complete plays. Below the bookcase, Down
Left, is a closet, the door of which opens out. When this door is
open, it blocks anyone inside the closet. Near the closet, Left
Center, is a backless loveseat. Down far Right is the entrance
to the conference room, having no door. Upstage of this
entrance, on the Down Right wall, is a small, decorative
mirror above a liquor cabinet. On the cabinet are some
liquor bottles and glasses. Upstage of the liquor cabinet, on
the right wall, are two large double windows. On the wall
Upstage of the windows are several photographs underneath
a poster of a play. On all the walls around the office are
numerous other posters of past productions tastefully framed
and arranged. There is a shag rug on the floor below the desk.
It is a sunny, Saturday afternoon in September.

AT RISE: As the curtain rises, HELEN OSBORNE flies out of the
bathroom Up Right humming happily and goes down to her
desk. She's wearing an attractive hat and has on a red hair-
piece. She finishes fastening a pin into the hat as she surveys
her desk.

HELEN. *(behind desk)* Let's see ... contract ... offering ...
Equity rules... *(HELEN puts the items above in a tote bag she*
pulls out from behind her desk. She looks over the desk one last time,
opens her purse, powders her nose, picks up her tote bag, drops her
purse into it, and crosses to the door with the transom Up Left. She
pauses and looks in a wall mirror below the door. She fixes her hair,
fluffs it up, adjusts the hat, shakes her head watching the hair move,
gives it a final flourish and stands looking at herself critical-

ly.) No, no, no, no—! *(She removes the hat and the wig comes off with it revealing HELEN'S natural hair. She drops the hat/wig into her tote bag, gives her hair another quick fluff, shrugs, and opens the door. Suddenly remembering.)* The set sketches!

(She leaves the door half open and Exits into the conference room D.R. A beat. JAMES SKIPWORTH appears in the door and stands hesitantly looking in. Extremely anxious, he tentatively steps into the office. He carries a briefcase. JAMES looks around the office, glances at the posters on the walls and notices HELEN'S Tony on the desk. He crosses R. to the desk, hears a noise from the conference room, is paralyzed with fear. JAMES notices the open door leading to the bathroom and, on impulse, darts above the desk, Enters the bathroom door and closes it without making a noise. A beat. HELEN Enters from the conference room holding the sketches under her arm and crosses to the door U. L. As she's about to Exit, the TOILET FLUSHES. Puzzled, she takes several steps back into the office, staying U. L., as JAMES Enters from the bathroom.)

HELEN. *(sizing him up, suspiciously)* May I help you?

JAMES. *(U.R.C., behind desk)* What? *(His leg begins to shake.)*

HELEN. I said 'may I help you?' *(Takes a step to him.)*

JAMES. *(a step to her)* Mrs. Osborne?

HELEN. Yes?

JAMES. *(trying to smile)* My name is... *(JAMES'S leg shakes violently.)* I... I... *(After a superhuman effort to control his shaking without success, JAMES shrugs, then dashes back into the bathroom and slams the door. A puzzled HELEN stands looking after him for a long beat, then crosses R. to the bathroom door and knocks. She is stage L. of the door and partially facing front.)*

HELEN. *(above desk, sweetly)* Hellooooo?

JAMES. *(off stage, a beat)* Who is it?

HELEN. *(a look of disbelief)* Who is it? Did you say "who is it?"

JAMES. *(off stage)* WHAT?

HELEN. Wait a minute, let's start over. This is my office and you are someone who's in my bathroom. Who are you and what are you doing in there?

JAMES. *(off stage, another beat)* I'm thinking.

HELEN. Fine. You think, I'll call the police. *(She starts D. to the phone on the desk.)*

JAMES. *(off stage)* Who?

HELEN. *(Shouts at the bathroom door over her shoulder.)* THE POLICE! *(HELEN places her tote bag and set sketches on the chair behind the desk and picks up the receiver. The bathroom door rattles.)*

JAMES. *(off stage)* I'M COMING OUT! YOU DON'T HAVE TO CALL THE POLICE, I'M COMING OUT! *(The door rattles again.)*

HELEN. *(to herself:)* Wonderful. *(dialing)*

JAMES. *(off stage, rattling the door harder)* IT'S STUCK! I CAN'T GET IT OPEN! *(HELEN sighs, hangs up and steps back U.R. to the bathroom door.)*

HELEN. *(back to audience)* THAT'S A NEW DOOR! YOU PUSH, I'LL PULL! *(HELEN yanks hard on the door. It flies open and bumps her on the head.)* Ouch!

(JAMES steps out of the bathroom and stands sheepishly looking at HELEN who is above the desk, R. of JAMES.)

JAMES. Are you all right? *(He closes the bathroom door.)*

HELEN. *(touching her head gingerly)* No, damn it, my head hurts!

JAMES. *(a step to her)* I'm sorry, I'm really sorry...

HELEN. *(stepping quickly back)* Who are you? What are you doing here? *(HELEN'S suspicious step away from JAMES makes him even more nervous.)*

JAMES. I wanted to talk to you about... *(He clears his throat.)* Well. See, I called two days ago but your secretary said you were busy. I called last week and the week before that and I couldn't get to you on the phone so I dropped by yesterday and your secretary wouldn't let me in... *(He pauses, smiles with a sickly expression and shifts position nervously.)*

HELEN. *(HELEN snatches a Kleenex from the desk and dabs at her wound as she moves D. R. of the desk. Eyeing JAMES warily.)* Are you an actor? I don't see people without an appointment.

JAMES. No, I'm not. I'm a... *(JAMES turns and walks a few steps to L. of the desk.)* Well ... *(Clears his throat.)* ...I did some... in high school, but that was... I haven't... *(Turns to HELEN.)* ...I'm a...No. I'm not. An actor.

HELEN. Well. I'm certainly glad that's settled. So far this has been a terribly enlightening conversation.

JAMES. *(brightening, an eager step toward her.)* You think so?

HELEN. *(HELEN quickly holds her hands up as if to stop JAMES'S approach. A firm step away from him.)* Look, Mr...

JAMES. Skipworth. James Skipworth. *(His leg begins to shake.)*

HELEN. Mr. Skipworth, I don't have time to—

JAMES. *(Leans in over the desk and addresses HELEN*

intimately. Blurting.) You look better in person than you do on television do you mind if I do some push ups? *(Without waiting for an answer, JAMES drops his briefcase beside the left end of the desk and does ten quick pushups beside the desk as HELEN watches deadpan. JAMES finishes, hops to his feet and stands motionless looking at HELEN.)*

HELEN. *(A beat as they stand eyeing each other.)* Are you sick, Mr. Skipworth?

JAMES. *(distracted look)* What?

HELEN. *(carefully)* Are you sick? You look as though you're about to pass out.

JAMES. I'm not sure... *(JAMES begins running in place in a quick spurt, knees high, an intense look on his face, then breaks to D. L. and begins doing calesthenics. HELEN is fascinated.)*

HELEN. *(measuring him)* What are you doing?

JAMES. I'm hyper-active. When I get like this, I have to exercise. *(HELEN studies JAMES a moment, then crosses U. R. to her desk and picks up her Tony award from the desk to use as a weapon.)*

HELEN. *(on guard)* Mr. Skipworth? You still haven't told me why you're here.

JAMES. *(Stops exercising, thinks.)* Oh. Yeah. *(He tries to relax and casually begins to amble toward HELEN who is U R. of the desk.)* Well. I'm sorry to intrude, I mean, I know I made a bad impression, but this means a lot to me... *(He sees HELEN holding her Tony ready to strike, changes directions in mid-gait, and crosses back D. L. to above the love seat.)* I wanted to see you about...a...see, I...Oh, Boy!

HELEN. *(crossing D. R., keeping her distance)* What is it you want? Why don't you just come right out and say it?

JAMES. *(Turns to face her.)* I can't.

HELEN. *(firmly)* What do you mean, you can't? *(She moves toward him threateningly, accenting her words with Tony.)* You're leaving right now!

JAMES. *(Quickly crosses D. stage in front of HELEN, ending far D. R.)* No, no, I can't leave! Okay. Okay. I'll tell you exactly why I'm here. *(HELEN faces him squarely, eyes narrow. JAMES faces front.)* Okay. All right. *(Clears his throat.)* I'm a...I have a... (big sigh) ...This is so hard.

HELEN. *(now C. stage)* What is?

JAMES. Admitting that I'm a... *(Turns decisively to face her.)* Well okay, this is it. I'm a...I have a... *(barely audible)* ...play.

HELEN. What?

JAMES. A play. *(shrugging hopelessly)* I have a play.

HELEN. A play? You're a playwright?

JAMES. *(nodding, ashamed)* Yes.

HELEN. *(Relaxes, heaves a sigh of relief, laughs, and shakes her head.)* I should have known. *(She crosses U. L. to the door, depositing the Tony on the desk as she passes below it.)* Send in your script and I'll read it after I open my current production. Thank you for coming by. *(She holds the door open for JAMES.)*

JAMES. *(desperately)* I have it with me! *(Dashes below the desk to its L. side, snatches his briefcase from the floor, and begins to cross slowly U. L. to HELEN at the door as he fishes his play out of the briefcase.)*

HELEN. *(laying it out) Just leave it! (Then an attempt at being gracious:)* I'll get to it as soon as I can.

JAMES. *(Stops dead a few steps from her, his hand in his briefcase, and stares at HELEN.)* Leave it? You mean...just leave it?

HELEN. *(impatiently)* Yes, that's what I said. Just leave it. *(HELEN nods toward the desk. JAMES looks at the desk then back at HELEN, his face a mask of despair.)*

JAMES. *(big sigh)* All right. *(Takes a manilla envelope out of his briefcase and looks at HELEN, his misery evident.)* Where shall I... *(HELEN crosses briskly to him, snatches the envelope from his hands, goes below him to the desk and tosses the play haphazardly on a corner of the desk. She turns, marches L. above him back to the door and opens it wider. JAMES looks from HELEN to the desk twice. He notices the positioning of his script, steps to above the desk and places the envelope dead center on it. He turns to HELEN and gazes at her with helpless anguish.)*

HELEN. *(smiling sweetly)* Thank you for coming by.

JAMES. You're welcome. *(JAMES heaves another big sigh, turns and crosses reluctantly U. L. to the door as if he's wearing lead boots. He whimpers, seems about to say something, then with sudden conviction, goes past HELEN and out the door. HELEN closes the door behind him, leans with her back on the door, shakes her head and laughs, then crosses R. to above the desk. She picks up her purse from the chair, takes her compact out and checks her makeup. She tenderly powders the bump on her forehead, puts her compact back in her purse, picks up the tote bag with her left hand and grabs the set sketches with her right hand. She crosses back toward the door U. L. When she is halfway between the desk and the door, JAMES suddenly hurtles back in, drops his briefcase near the door, throws himself at HELEN'S feet and grabs her around the knees. He is on her left, his face facing the audience. Weeping openly.)* PLEASE! Produce my play! Oh GOD! You don't know what this MEANS to me! Give me a production, somewhere, ANYWHERE! Broadway, Off-Broadway, MONTAUK POINT!

HELEN. *(facing front, looking down at JAMES in a surprisingly calm and steady voice)* Mr. Skipworth?

JAMES. I CAN'T STAND IT ANYMORE! I'm drowning in rejection!

HELEN. *(clutching her tote bag and sketches close to her)* Mr. Skipworth...

JAMES. I'm suffocating in anonymity! *(He jerks his head up to her but keeps his arms locked around her knees.)* What's wrong with me?

HELEN. May I say something here?! May I—

JAMES. *(barreling through)* —Am I under some kind of curse?—

HELEN. *(struggling to get free)* —Mr. Skipworth, you're mashing my knees—

JAMES. —Am I writing in Sanscrit? I'm not getting through! *(HELEN almost breaks free but JAMES makes a lunge for her and again locks his arms around her legs.)*

HELEN. HEY, YOU!? HEY! HEY!! You're staining my Gucci's!

JAMES. What? What?

HELEN. My Gucci's, my GUCCI'S! *(laying it out)* STOP-CRYING-ON-MY-GUCCI'S! My God, don't you know how destructive SALT is?!

JAMES. I'm sorry, I'm sorry— *(Pulls a square of toilet tissue out of his sports jacket pocket and dabs blindly at HELEN'S shoes with it.)*

HELEN. *(inching slowly toward the desk sideways with tiny steps)* Try to get control of yourself! *(JAMES moves with her on his knees, his arms still clutching her lower legs.)*

JAMES. *(Louder sobs.)* Yes...yes...I am...I'm trying...

HELEN. *(fighting for control)* Be strong! Be a man! Be a—

JAMES. I'm sorry, you just don't know what it's like, I mean, I'm so FRUSTRATED!

HELEN. *(close to the desk, still inching along)* Give your typewriter a COLD SHOWER! *(She stops moving, drops her gaze to him and shouts.)* HEY, YOU! YOU'RE GRINDING MY KNEES TO A PULP!

JAMES. *(loosening his grasp)* I'm sorry, I'm sorry, I'm—

HELEN. —Let go of me!

JAMES. NO!

HELEN. *(striking at him with her tote bag)* Let go of me or I'll scream! *(HELEN abruptly stops pounding on JAMES, looks front, pauses, then screams. The scream is brief but loud. HELEN'S scream startles JAMES. He loosens his hold on her legs. She breaks free and runs U. R. to the desk. JAMES remains on his knees U. C., L. of the desk.)* Stay away! Stay away from me or I'll—*(behind the desk)* —I'll call the police! *(HELEN tosses her tote bag, purse and set sketches on the chair and snatches the receiver off the hook.*

JAMES. *(suddenly calm)* Call the police? I'm not a criminal. I'm a writer. *(JAMES rises facing stage R., then humbly:)* Just promise to produce my play, that's all I want.

HELEN. *(Stops with the phone half way to her ear.)* Promise to produce your play? Are you crazy? How can I promise that? I told you I'll read it when I get time!

JAMES. *(throwing his arms wildly)* You won't read it!

HELEN. I will, I swear it! I'm very good about reading plays.

JAMES. Oh, really? *(Goes to left of the desk and grabs an unopened manilla envelope off the top of the pile. Reading the postmark.)* July! Three months ago.

HELEN. *(evasively)* In July I had a lot of scripts to learn for "THE WILLFUL AND THE WANTON." *(She hangs up the receiver.)*

JAMES. *(skeptically)* Uh, huh.

HELEN. *(hands on hips defiantly, facing stage L.)* What do you mean, 'uh huh?' The character I play was put on trial for murder, got involved in three affairs, and had her tubes tied!

JAMES. *(leafing through envelopes)* August...July...June—

HELEN. *(Drops her gaze and studies her nails defensively.)* In June I produced VIRGINIA WOLF at Hyannis Port...

JAMES. *(leafing through unopened manuscripts)* March ...December, 9 months ago! *(Holds up the envelope and pinions HELEN with an accusing stare.)*

HELEN. I don't have to justify my life to you! *(Crosses D. R. of the desk, grabs the envelope from JAMES and throws it back on the desk.)* Look. I told you, I'll read your play when I have—

JAMES. *(crossing U. L. of the desk)* You won't read it and you won't produce it. You're only trying to placate me because you think I'm a looney! *(JAMES begins pacing up and down stage L. during the following:)*

HELEN. *(placating, trying a new, conciliatory tone)* I don't think you're a "looney." I think you're... *(careful selection)* ...very upset and frustrated which I can certainly understand and sympathize with, but you must be reasonable about this. Now, just slow down and try and get control of your *(Clears her throat.)* ...motor responses.

JAMES. Yes, you're right, I'll try. I'll try. *(Stops pacing, squints his eyes closed, clenches his fists and holds a beat. He finally gives up, does 10 quick pushups and continues pacing.)*

HELEN. *(now U. C., behind the desk, impatiently:)* Think about something peaceful like... *(sweeping gesture with her hands)* majestic mountains...

JAMES. I'm afraid of heights.

HELEN. ...green fields...

JAMES. *(still pacing)* I'm allergic to ragweed.

HELEN. *(flat, with disdain)* How about a cesspool in Secaucus? *(JAMES doesn't respond.)* Have you tried meditation?

JAMES. *(shaking head, throws her a look as he paces.)* I can't cross my legs. Besides, I'd rather write.

HELEN. Yes, I'm sure you would. *(Distracted, HELEN looks at her watch.)* Are you feeling better?

JAMES. No.

HELEN. *(She begins picking up her tote bag and sketches from the chair during the following.)* Good, that's good. Just try to relax and—

JAMES. *(Now D. L., he turns and faces her.)* Relax? How can I relax when I get constant rejection and I can't even get an agent?

HELEN. *(studying a sketch)* Yes...this business is a meat grinder. Ninety per cent of the people in it end up steak tartar.

JAMES. *(head hanging, tragically)* I know, I know.

HELEN. Good. *(tucking the sketches under her arm)* Why don't you come with me now and we'll leave together. *(She starts toward the door U. L.)*

JAMES. *(D. L., turns to HELEN and delivers the line with rising inflection:)* I'm not leaving until I get a commitment!

HELEN. *(Stops U. C., half way to the door.)* What?

JAMES. *(tortured)* I'm not leaving until I get a commitment.

HELEN. *(fixing JAMES with a level gaze)* All right. Enough games. *(She crosses back R. to behind desk.)* Let's put an end to this right now. *(Picks up the receiver and begins dialing, trying to manage the phone, the tote bag and sketches all at once.)*

JAMES. *(Crosses to the door U. L., picks up his briefcase and stands it against the wall U. of the door.)* Okay. I didn't want to do this, but you leave me no choice. I'll have to do it. I don't want to but I have to! *(Notices the door is half open.)*

HELEN. What are you talking about?

JAMES. I'll have to resort to blackmail. *(Puts his hand on the doorknob.)*

HELEN. *(laughs)* Blackmail? *(Finishes dialing and looks quizzically at JAMES as she waits for someone to answer her call.)*

JAMES. I'll tell your husband you're having an affair with your lawyer. *(Slams the door shut on the word "lawyer.")*

HELEN. *(Looks at JAMES in astonishment, then places the sketches on the desk without breaking eye contact.)* What did you say?

JAMES. *(Leans casually against the door and crosses his arms.)* I happen to know you're having an affair with your lawyer, Sidney Meyer.

HELEN. That's the most ridiculous thing I've ever heard! *(a beat, then:)* Where did you get such an absurd idea?

JAMES. Sidney Meyer lives at 822 West End Avenue, northeast corner apartment, third floor. *(JAMES uncrosses his arms and ambles D. R. going below the desk.)* Last night, as on many previous nights, I observed you enter Mr. Meyer's apartment at 11:48 and leave this morning at 8:15 wearing glasses and a red wig. *(JAMES throws a look at HELEN on the the word 'wig' as he continues crossing D. R.)*

HELEN. *(self-consciously stuffing her red wig further down in her tote bag.)* I don't even own a red wig!

JAMES. *(has his back to her, looking out the double windows)* I assume you were trying to disguise yourself so that none of your fans from the soap opera would recognize you.

HELEN. *(Hangs up, then studies JAMES intensely.)* Did Scott hire you? Are you a private detective?

JAMES. *(still gazing out the window)* No. I told you, I'm a writer. I live in Mr. Meyer's building... *(a forlorn look front)* ...one room, basement apartment, pipes everywhere, ceiling flaking off...

HELEN. Well, Mr. Skipworth...

JAMES. *(continuing morosely)* ...running toilet, view of a fireplug...

HELEN. ...one thing I detest is threats and they don't frighten me. *(She picks up the phone and as she continues speaking, goes right of the desk to JAMES at the window.)* Go ahead. Call my husband. *(HELEN'S ploy catches JAMES off guard. He stands staring at her. Left of JAMES.)* Go ahead. Call him. Here. *(She hands the phone to him.)*

JAMES. *(Hesitates, then takes it. Faking casualness.)* Okay. Sure. Good. That's just what I'm going to do. I'll call him. *(Holds up the phone.)* On the phone.

HELEN. *(smiling)* Yes, if you're going to call him, I suggest you use a phone. Go ahead. *(HELEN folds her arms and taps her foot as she stares hard at JAMES. JAMES clears his throat, then, holding the phone with his left hand, takes out a piece of paper from his left inside jacket pocket. HELEN tries to see the number but JAMES shields it by clutching it to his chest.)*

JAMES. *(crossing above HELEN to C. stage)* You may not believe me, Mrs. Osborne, but I detest doing this. I'm really a very fine person.

HELEN. Hah! *(She turns and watches him, arms still folded.)*

JAMES. *(C. stage, studying the number as if it's hard to read)* In high school I was voted the guy who was the least likely to cheat on his income tax. And I haven't cheated…either of the years I filed. *(JAMES picks up the receiver, wedges it between his cheek and shoulder, and dials/punches the number quickly.)*

HELEN. *(taking two steps L. toward him)* How did you get my number? It's unlisted.

JAMES. *(Finishes dialing.)* I have a friend who works for the phone company. *(JAMES looks at HELEN, then smiles with a sickly expression. Into the receiver.)* Hello? Mr. Osborne, it is my sad duty to inform you that your wife Helen is having an affair with her lawyer, Sidney Meyer— *(He is interrupted, listens, then nods and speaks louder.)* I said your wife is having an affair with her lawyer, Sidney— *(He listens, nods.)* Yes, I observed her going into Sid's apartment— *(Listens.)* Sid, he's— *(Nods.)* I'm sorry, I'll speak louder. *(shouting into receiver:)* IT'S YOUR WIFE, HELEN. SHE'S HAVING AN AFFAIR— *(Shakes head 'no.')* Who I am isn't important… *(Listens.)* No, I am not

SIDNEY MEYER, I'm... *(Listens.)* This isn't a joke! *(Holds the phone at arms length and winces, then puts the receiver back to his ear and listens. to HELEN:)* Wrong number. *(Hangs up.)*

HELEN. Even if you'd dialed the right number, you wouldn't have reached Scott. He's on the west coast shooting a commercial.

JAMES. Oh.

HELEN. *(HELEN glances quickly at her watch, then during her following lines, crosses up to above the desk and begins to gather her things as JAMES crosses U. C. to the desk.)* Look, Mr. Skipworth, I'm due at Sardi's. I suggest we end this farce. You can do whatever you want with your information. Tell Scott, don't tell Scott, he wouldn't care anyway. So. Shall we go? *(HELEN tosses her tote bag over her shoulder.)*

JAMES. No. *(He puts the phone down on the right edge of the desk, while part of the extension cord remains D. L. of the desk.)*

HELEN. Yes! *(HELEN is still behind the desk. She snatches the set sketches angrily.*

JAMES. *(Crosses D. and begins pacing furiously.)* You don't know what this means to me! This is a crisis in my life! You're my last hope— *(JAMES stops D. R. and gazes at the ceiling as if searching for inspiration.)* You're the ladder on which I would climb into the sunshine of a better day.

HELEN. *(Walks around left of the desk to D. L. C., facing JAMES who is D. R.)* Mr. Skipworth, for your information, I never let anyone climb me before six o'clock. May we go?

JAMES. *(Turns, looks at HELEN with a wild expression.)* You haven't heard a word I said. Don't you have any compassion? *(The following lines rush out with overlaps and building anger.)*

HELEN. *(D. L C.)* Not on Saturday.

JAMES. *(D. R.)* Don't you see this distraught mass of humanity writhing before you?

HELEN. *(a step R. toward him)* I told you I'll read your play—

JAMES. *(A step L toward her)* —I don't believe you! I need to have you promise to give me a production—

HELEN. *(another step toward him)* —Do you really expect me to promise to produce a play I haven't even read?

JAMES. *(another step to her)* Yes I do! I demand it!! For once in my life, I DEMAND something!

HELEN. You can demand all you want. I won't do it!

JAMES. *(Falls to his knees.)* Please? PLEASE?

HELEN. *(shouting to the ceiling)* STOP GROVELING.

JAMES. *(Suddenly sober, JAMES looks at HELEN, rises with all the dignity he can muster, and goes D. R. He stops, then turns to her.)* If you don't I have to kill myself by five o'clock. *(HELEN glances quickly at her wristwatch.)*

HELEN. How about making it two thirty?

JAMES. *(matter-of-fact)* I've taken a suicide vow.

HELEN. That's ridiculous. I'm getting out of here! *(HELEN starts for the door U. L as JAMES runs above the love seat and places himself between her and her only means of escape.)*

JAMES. *(as he runs)* No it isn't! It isn't ridiculous! I swore if I didn't get a play produced by five o'clock on my forty second birth, I'd kill myself. Today is my forty second birthday!

HELEN. Happy birthday. *(She steps L. to get around JAMES but he blocks her way. Overlap lines.)*

JAMES. You don't believe me.

HELEN. You're standing in my way. *(Steps to her R.)*

JAMES. *(blocking her way)* If I didn't do this, I'd never get over my inhibitions...

HELEN. —Mr. Skipworth—

JAMES. —I'd never gotten out of my room... *(He puts his hands on her shoulders.)*

HELEN. *(shouting)* What are you doing?

JAMES. I don't want to die there anonymously!

HELEN. Get out of my way! *(pushing JAMES toward the door)*

JAMES. *(standing defiantly with his back against the door, his arms clutching the door sides)* NOT UNTIL I GET A COMMITMENT!

HELEN. *(HELEN suddenly changes her attitude and stares at JAMES for a beat. Then:)* Okay.

JAMES: Okay?

HELEN. If you get out of my way, I promise I'll produce it.

JAMES. *(Pauses, warily.)* Why are you promising to produce a play you haven't read?

HELEN. *(Crosses to the love seat D. L.)* Because I have a hunch about you. I'm sure your play is good. *(She puts the sketches on the love seat.)* You have a kind of inner intensity, a crazy determination that could be genius.

JAMES. *(Goes D. L. to left of HELEN.)* Really?

HELEN. *(to him:)* Yes. *(Looks front, pauses.)* It could also be an imbalance in your hormones... *(Looks at JAMES.)* ...but I think it's genius. *(JAMES'S leg begins to shake.)*

JAMES. Genius?

HELEN. *(Opens her purse.)* I'll take an option on your play right now.

JAMES. You will?

HELEN. *(Takes out a checkbook.)* This... *(Waves checkbook.)* ...is a checkbook. *(HELEN fishes for a pen. JAMES whips one out of his inside left jacket pocket, steps over and hands it to her.)* Thank you. *(writing)* Two hundred...fifty dollars...and no...etcetera...there. *(She rips the check out and gives it to JAMES.)*

JAMES. *(Takes the check and studies it, then to HELEN:)* You're trying to trick me.

HELEN. *(innocently)* No I'm not. *(She drops the pen and checkbook into her purse.)*

JAMES. *(wanting to believe it)* You could stop payment on this.

HELEN. *(Puts her purse back into her tote bag.)* I wouldn't do that. *(Smiles graciously at JAMES.)*

JAMES. Well... *(He stuffs the check in his outside left handkerchief pocket with part of the check remaining visible.)* ...I'd like you to read my play right now.

HELEN. *(crossing D. R. C., in front of the love seat)* No!!! I'm not going to read it now! I have to be at Sardi's in twenty minutes! *(She turns, faces JAMES.)* Don't you understand that?

JAMES. Sure, but you...

HELEN. *(low, controlled fury with hands clenched on the strap of her tote bag)* I'm meeting a wealthy investor by the name of John Fowler. Mr. Fowler may come up with the final one hundred twenty five thousand for my current play. We're supposed to start previews next week and if I don't get the money today, I'll have to close down the production and take a loss! It's absolutely imperative that I be there and I have to be on time because Mr. Fowler is a stickler for punctuality! *(She goes L. to the love seat, snatches up the sketches, and starts for the up L. door.)* I have to go. Now! *(JAMES counters HELEN by sprinting U. stage past her to the door. He turns, blocking her way with a defiant look. HELEN stops L, a few steps from the door.)* Let me out of this office or I'm calling the police and pressing charges! *(JAMES doesn't budge.)* Very well. *(She crosses R. to above the desk.)*

JAMES. Please, Mrs. Osborne, don't do that! *(HELEN picks up the receiver and starts to dial a number. JAMES runs D. L. of the desk, picks up the extension cord of the phone, and yanks it. The phone, including the receiver in HELEN'S hand, flies off the desk and onto the floor in front of her.)*

HELEN. *(Stares at the phone on the floor, then a slow take to JAMES.)* All right, Mr. Playwright, now you've really done it. I'll never read your play, much less produce it. *(She storms L. below the desk to JAMES, grabs the check from his coat pocket. Then, waving the check in his face:)* And what's more, I'll see to it that no other producer produces your play...ever! *(Taps him on the nose with the check.)* You've come in here, raved... *(Tears check in two.)* ...threatened... *(Tears again.)* ...and cried on my Gucci's! *(Rips it into pieces and throws them in the air.)* You're a crazy person!

JAMES. I am not!

HELEN. *(waving her U. finger in his face.)* Yes you are!

JAMES. All I want you to do is read my—

HELEN. Crazy, crazy, crazy, CRAZY! *(HELEN feints to the R. When JAMES steps in her way, she goes L. around him and dashes to the door U. L, getting it partially opened before JAMES arrives behind her and prevents her from opening it further. HELEN'S mouth is pressed against the crack.)* Crazy! There's a CRAZY person in here! Help! HELP!

JAMES. *(Slams the door shut.)* Mrs. Osborne...

HELEN. *(pounding on door)* Crazy! Crazy! Somebody HELP ME! *(She yanks on the doorknob but JAMES holds it shut.)*

JAMES. Mrs. Osborne, will you please get away from the door?

HELEN. This is my door! Don't tell me what to do to my own DOOR!

JAMES. If you don't, I'll have to take drastic action.

HELEN. Get away from that door! *(Pushes him.)*

JAMES. No!

HELEN. Yes! *(Pushes him again.)*

JAMES. No!

HELEN. YES, YES!!! *(Pushes him twice.)*

JAMES. *(JAMES grabs his briefcase which is resting just above the door against the wall and takes out a two-headed hammer. He brandishes it comically at HELEN.)* Aggghhh!

HELEN. *(Backs up in horror.)* Don't you threaten me!

JAMES. *(growling, waving the hammer)* Grrrr! GRRR-RRRRR!!! *(HELEN freezes. She screams, then runs to her desk and stands behind it so that the desk is between herself and JAMES at the U. L. door.)*

HELEN. I don't care what you do! I'm never going to read your play! Nevernevernever!!!! *(JAMES reaches into his briefcase, takes out some nails and begins nailing the door shut. Three or four pre-drilled holes will enable him to push the nails in with his left hand while he pounds the hammer on the door next to the nails, thus giving the illusion of driving the nails in. These should be large nails, visible to the audience. HELEN is still behind desk.)* What are you doing? Hey! HEY!! What do you think you're — STOP THAT! STOP IT!! I said — *(sudden realization)* Oh, my God, I'll be trapped in here with a madman! *(HELEN charges impulsively toward the door crossing above the desk. JAMES turns and brandishes the hammer. HELEN stops in her tracks halfway between the desk and the door, screams, and runs behind the desk. JAMES turns back to the door and finishes angling nails into the door and frame. He turns around and looks at HELEN who stares back, shaking, from behind the desk. She sees the phone on the floor below the desk and dashes down to it. JAMES beats her, picks it up and brandishes the hammer again. HELEN screams, darts back behind the stage R. end of desk and stands staring at JAMES, panting. After a long, tense pause.)* Do I understand that you intend to force me to stay here until I agree to produce your play?

JAMES. *(D. L, facing her)* Yes.

HELEN. You must know that will never work. *(She carefully puts the set sketches down on the desk.)* You cannot force someone to produce something they don't want to produce. *(Carefully places tote bag on desk, then, hands on desk, she leans toward JAMES; great intensity:)* And what's to prevent me from reading your play, agreeing to what you want, and then having you arrested when you let me out?

JAMES. I've thought of that. *(Scratches back with the hammer.)* My only hope is that I can reach you on the one common ground shared by all producers.

HELEN. Which is?

JAMES. Greed. *(pointing at HELEN with hammer)* I have to convince you that my play will make so much money, you can't afford to pass it up. *(Sticks the hammer in his belt.)*

HELEN. But why me, of all producers?

JAMES. *(Crosses to stage L. of desk and places the phone on the left front end of desk.)* You're the only one I have a personal contact with.

HELEN. What personal contact? *(Hands on stage L. end of desk, JAMES leans in toward HELEN who is still leaning in on stage R. end of desk.)*

JAMES. You're having an affair with someone who lives in my building.

HELEN. *(Throws her hands up in exasperation and crosses D. R., checking her watch as she goes. L. of liquor cabinet, HELEN turns, faces JAMES.)* Look. I have to be at Sardi's. My meeting's at four o'clock but I was supposed to meet Sid early and go over my presentation.

JAMES. *(high energy)* You'll make the four o'clock meeting if you start.— *(Suddenly stops mid-sentence, remembers something, looks at his watch. Politely, to HELEN.)* May I please use your phone, Mrs. Osborne?

HELEN. What?

JAMES. *(Crosses D. L.)* There's a sickness in my family. I asked my landlady to babysit. I want to see if everything's all right.

HELEN. *(D. R.)* What if I said no?

JAMES. I'll pay you for it... *(JAMES reaches into his pocket and pulls his hand out, empty.)* I'll give you an I.O.U.

HELEN. *(Hands to head.)* Wait a minute, just wait a minute. Everything's happening too fast. I'm trying to assimilate what's going on here. *(She walks slowly D. R.)* Now, you just asked calmly and politely if you could use my phone. Right? *(Turns, looks at JAMES.)*

JAMES. Yes?

HELEN. *(Walks slowly back and forth, D. R., thinking it through.)* But a few minutes ago you nailed my door shut and threatened me with a hammer. *(to JAMES:)* You can see why I'm just a little confused by your behavior.

JAMES. *(Takes a few steps U. stage to stay parallel with HELEN.)* Certainly. I'm confused too. I never thought I could do anything like this. I've always been very shy. *(Looks front lost in thought.)*

HELEN. *(HELEN sees JAMES is not watching and angles U. C. toward the phone on the L. side of the desk during the following:)* Why is it always the shy ones who go berserk? Three weeks ago the writer of my current production, who was also shy, was here discussing a scene revision which I'd suggested. For no apparent reason, he went mad, tore up my office and ran screaming down the hall. *(HELEN is almost to the phone on the desk. JAMES turns his head and sees her. HELEN abruptly changes direction and crosses around the stage R. corner of the desk to U. R. behind desk.)*

JAMES. What happened to him?

HELEN. I think he's in Haiti. I've been receiving dolls of myself... *(She opens the desk drawer and takes out a doll with huge pins sticking through it. JAMES crosses up to HELEN behind desk and pulls a pin out of the doll.)*

JAMES. These are big pins.

HELEN. *(Disgusted by the doll.)* Make your call. *(She tosses the doll carelessly back into the drawer and slams it shut.)*

JAMES. Thank you. *(JAMES picks up the phone, takes it D. L. and sits on the love seat, facing front. As JAMES dials, HELEN picks up a sheet of paper from the desk and hastily writes an S.O.S. message on it.)* I really like you as a redhead.

HELEN. *(distracted, writing)* What?

JAMES. *(still dialing, facing front)* When you left Sid's apartment this morning you were wearing a red wig. You looked great. *(He throws HELEN a look over his shoulder.)*

HELEN. *(HELEN looks up from her writing, sees JAMES looking at her, quickly covers the note with her arm and smiles at him.)* Thank you.

JAMES. I know you probably think I'm a jackass for what I'm— *(into receiver)* Oh, Mrs. Heinkle! I wasn't calling you a jackass, I was talking to— *(listens)* Hello? Hello? *(JAMES depresses the button and quickly dials the number again as HELEN continues writing. She finishes and during the following, tries making a glider of the note. Into receiver.)* Hello, Mrs. Heinkle, don't hang up, this is James— *(listens)* That was me, I was talking to someone here— *(listens)* Jackass is in the dictionary, Mrs. Heinkle, it's in the common usage, it's like the word "piss." it's also in the diction— *(listens)* Hello? *(JAMES sighs and dials again. HELEN'S glider is finished. She tries making it fly but it nose dives into the floor. She picks up the note and tries making a second glider as JAMES gets through again. JAMES is on the love seat, facing D.)* James again, Mrs. Heinkle, PLEASE don't hang up! I just want to check and see how Susie's doing... *(Listens, then leans forward anxiously.)* She what? *(Listens, then registers profound shock.)* What do you mean? *(Listens, shakes head bewildered.)* How could she just... *(Listens, shakes head.)* Mrs. Heinkle, don't tell me that. *(Listens, near tears.)* No...I just won't accept that... *(HELEN has made a flyable version of a paper airplane and has edged to the window U. R. She tries to open it but it's stuck.)*

JAMES. *(moaning)* No...no...oh, no—! *(Covers his face with his hands and begins to sob.)*

HELEN. *(back to him, tugging on the U. stage window)* **What's the matter?** *(No answer from JAMES, only heart-rending sobs.)* **What's happened?** *(HELEN pounds around the edges of the window.)* **Open, damn it, OPEN!**

JAMES. *(through his sobs)* **It's Susie. She...she...** *(Breaks down into uncontrollable wailing.)*

HELEN. *(HELEN is struggling with the window. She throws JAMES a look over her shoulder, tugs again at the window, then looks back to JAMES. It registers that he's really crying. She abandons her efforts to open the window, crosses D. past the stage R. end of the desk and goes to JAMES at the love seat. Sympathetically.)* **Somebody...died?**

JAMES. *(nodding, not looking up)* **She'd only been sick a few hours...** *(loud sob)* **Mrs. Heinkle did everything she could...**

HELEN. **I'm sorry.** *(HELEN is touched by JAMES'S grief. At first she resists the impulse to comfort, but gives in to it and pats JAMES on the head.)*

JAMES. *(rocking back and forth)* **Before Susie it was Joann, then it was Roger, and before Roger it was Emelda.** *(JAMES looks up at HELEN who is on his R.)* **You know, hamsters don't live very long.**

HELEN. **Susie was...a hamster?** *(Her patting slows.)*

JAMES. *(nodding)* **Yes.** *(HELEN'S last pat on JAMES'S head is a disgusted slap. JAMES is looking front, dazed.)* **I used to give her little slices of apple. She'd eat them like watermelon. And she wasn't like the others...Susie never ate her babies!** *(wails)*

HELEN. *(a beat)* **Why don't you get a sea turtle? It'll outlive you by a hundred years.** *(HELEN slowly crosses D. R.)* **James. First things first.** *(Stops D. R., turns to him.)* **Think** of Susie. She needs you now, she needs a proper burial.

JAMES. *(looking front, sobs diminishing)* Mrs. Heinkle flushed her down the toilet.

HELEN. *(Looks front.)* How thoughtful.

JAMES. *(looking R. at HELEN, through subdued sobs)* Susie's probably half way to the Hudson River by now.

HELEN. *(Looks at him, then with a caustic edge:)* Well, if you hurry, you could hold a quick service for her as she passes under Riverside Drive. *(JAMES holds on HELEN a beat, then cries with renewed vigor.)* Mr. Skipworth, I'm sure that now, with your tragedy, you must see that what you're doing is unworthy of you.

JAMES. *(to her:)* You don't like to see me cry?

HELEN. No. I don't like to see you keeping me here.

JAMES. Oh.

HELEN. *(a step toward him)* Let me go.

JAMES. *(recovering)* I can't. *(Blows nose.)* I haven't changed my mind about you producing my play. I'm going to keep you here if it takes all night. *(HELEN turns front, shudders, crosses R. to the liquor cabinet, quickly pours a drink into a shot glass and gulps it down. Her eyes widen, she coughs, then faces JAMES decisively.)*

HELEN. *(hoarse whisper)* Mr. Skipworth... *(Clears throat.)* I've reconsidered my option money offer. I'll go as high as five hundred.

JAMES. *(still on love seat)* You're trying to bribe me.

HELEN. No I'm not.

JAMES. I'm not interested.

HELEN. *(Crosses L. to him, looking at her watch.)* Five fifty...no, six hundred dollars! I won't stop payment on it. My word as a producer. *(pause, then front)* My word as a human being.

JAMES. *(front, with determination)* No. You have to read it first. *(He looks at HELEN.)*

HELEN. All right. *(eyeing phone hungrily)* If you're not going to take the money, let me call Sid and tell him I'll be late. Please?

JAMES. *(rises)* I'll call for you. What's the number? *(He crosses up to L. of desk.)*

HELEN. *(following him)* 555-8422.

JAMES. *(Places the phone on the L. side of the desk and dials. Into receiver.)* Hello? I'm leaving a message for—

HELEN. *(casually)* Sidney Meyer. *(She crosses behind him to above the desk but hovers near phone.)*

JAMES. *(below her, on her L., looking front, into receiver)* Sidney Meyer, tell him Helen Osborne has been delayed, she'll be there later... *(Looks at her.)* If she reads my play. *(HELEN lunges across the desk, grabs the receiver with both hands, and shouts into it.)*

HELEN. *(in one breath)* Help! Henri, call the POLICE! I've been kidnapped by an INSANE PLAYWRIGHT who's TOTALLY BERSERK—! *(JAMES depresses the button. HELEN hears the click and sees JAMES'S finger on the disconnect button. She looks at him, smiles superficially and hands him the receiver. JAMES hangs up. A long pause. HELEN is still behind the desk.)* Mr. Skipworth, I don't think you fully understand my situation. *(She goes around the stage L. side of the desk and comes down to JAMES who is just below it.)* Let's take a little stroll, shall we?

JAMES. Okay.

HELEN. *(Above and just ahead of JAMES, holding his left arm, she moves him slowly stage L. as she talks.)* Now. *(slowly and carefully)* I know you're a writer and have very little awareness of the business end of producing. *(Looks at him.)* Am I correct?

JAMES. *(to her:)* Well...yes.

`HELEN. *(still moving L.)* All right. But you are cognizant of the fact that to produce a play...does take money?

JAMES. *(nodding vigorously)* Sure.

HELEN. *(Stops both of them U. L., then, praising the child:)* Very good, Mr. Skipworth. I do see a glimmer of hope in all this. *(JAMES smiles at HELEN. She smiles back politely, then indicates their next direction by pointing D. R. JAMES is just above HELEN and ahead of her as they begin crossing to the D. R. area.)* Now. I'm going to tell you something in confidence. Just between the two of us. Do I make myself clear?

JAMES. *(Stops C. stage. HELEN stops with him. Then, to her:)* Yes. It's a secret.

HELEN. Excellent. Excellent! You're following me better than most writers would, Mr. Skipworth. I'm very impressed with your quick grasp of a difficult subject.

JAMES. *(beaming)* Thank you.

HELEN. *(confidentially, continuing their cross D. R.)* The secret is this. I am under-financed in my current production.

JAMES. *(Eyes glued to her.)* Yeah?

HELEN. *(looking at floor, thoughtfully)* Yeah. That means I don't have enough money.

JAMES. Okay.

HELEN. *(studying his face)* You with me so far?

JAMES. *(thoughtfully chewing on his lower lip)* I think so.

HELEN. Good. *(They've arrived D. R. Now slightly above him, she begins to lead him stage L.)* Now. It's absolutely imperative that I have one hundred twenty five thousand big ones in the bank by Monday.

JAMES. *(stops, stunned)* One hundred twenty five thousand dollars?

HELEN. *(Continues three steps ahead of JAMES, then stops, turns back to him.)* You're very quick. Now, if I—

JAMES. *(on her R.)* What happens if you don't?

HELEN. *(holding C. stage, facing stage R.)* I'll have to close the production and take a terrible financial beating, not to mention what it will do to my reputation in the business...

JAMES. *(facing her)* Uh huh...

HELEN. *(growing more confident that she may be getting through)* If the show closes, it would hurt a lot of people, including you.

JAMES. Me?

HELEN. Yes. I'll have great difficulty raising money for my future productions. *(HELEN crosses R. to JAMES, takes his arm and lays this out emphatically.)* I-wouldn't-be-able-to-produce-your-play.

JAMES. *(Looks from HELEN front.)* Oh. *(HELEN continues leading him across stage to D. L.)*

HELEN. Now. I told you about the important backer I'm meeting at four, but I was due fifteen minutes ago to talk to Sid first...

JAMES. *(R. of HELEN, stops)* Okay.

HELEN. *(facing him)* Okay? You mean I can go?

JAMES. No. I mean okay, we'd better get started.

(HELEN looks at JAMES with dismay as JAMES crosses U. to the desk.) If you read fast, you can be out of here by three thirty.

HELEN. *(Stamps her foot.)* No!

JAMES. *(At desk, picks up manila envelope holding his play.)* You're the one who's holding things up. *(Examines envelope to be sure it's his.)* I told them at Sardi's you'd be a little late. You have time to read it.

HELEN. *(Hands to head in frustration.)* I can't concentrate on a play!

JAMES. *(At desk, turns, faces C.)* Think of something peaceful. Apply your emotional brake. Try meditation.

HELEN. *(pacing D. L, shooting him a look)* Don't give me that garbage!

JAMES. Mrs. Osborne, now, just sit down... *(Indicates couch against U. C. wall.)* Kick off your shoes...relax... *(Holds up his play.)* This is my play... *(Crosses D. L to HELEN.)* I'm bringing it over to you...

HELEN. *(Checks her watch, looks at JAMES, pauses, then makes a decision.)* All right, all right. You win, Mr. Skipworth.

JAMES. *(stage R. of HELEN)* Huh?

HELEN. I said you win. If it means this much to you, if you can go this far, then maybe you do have something. I'll read your play.

JAMES. *(Studies HELEN a beat.)* You're serious. You're really serious!

HELEN. *(sighs wearily)* Yes, I am.

JAMES. *(overjoyed)* I don't believe it! *(pacing D. C.)* I didn't think it would work. I thought—! I don't know what I thought, I didn't think you'd...but I got through to you!

HELEN. *(with an edge of sarcasm)* Well, you have put me in somewhat of a bind. *(sighs)* However, I am reachable. I can be moved, Mr. Skipworth. *(Runs hands through hair.)* I am human.

JAMES. *(nods)* You're very compassionate.

HELEN. *(two beats then front)* I know.

JAMES. I think it's your compassion that makes you so believable on THE WILLFUL AND THE WANTON.

HELEN. *(Picks up immediately. to JAMES:)* Do you watch it?

JAMES. All the time. It's the best soap opera on TV. I think you're a fantastic actress.

HELEN. *(graciously, as to a fan)* Thank you.

JAMES. And you have a lot of charisma.

HELEN. *(charmed)* Give me the play. *(Holds out her hand.)*

JAMES. Okay. *(JAMES starts eagerly L. toward HELEN, then stops dead, staring at her.)* I just had a horrible thought.

HELEN. What? What is it?

JAMES. *(Turns R. and moves away from her.)* After all I've gone through, what if you don't like it?

HELEN. That's always a possibility.

JAMES. *(Stops D. R., facing front.)* Maybe I'm just deluding myself. Maybe I can't write.

HELEN. *(with some tolerance)* Look. Give me the play. Let me be the judge.

JAMES. *(Turns to her.)* If you hate it, will you be kind?

HELEN. *(Crosses R. to JAMES.)* I'm not vicious but I am

honest. If I like it, it doesn't necessarily mean it's good. If I don't like it, it doesn't mean it's bad. It's just my opinion.

JAMES. *(nodding thoughtfully)* That's true. It's only an opinion. *(JAMES'S leg starts to shake.)*

HELEN. That's all it is.

JAMES. *(to her, relieved smile)* There's nothing to be afraid of.

HELEN. Nothing. *(Holds out hand.)* Now, give me the play.

JAMES. *(still smiling)* No.

HELEN. *(angry, two steps L.)* This is incredible! *(Turns back to him.)* You're the most insecure man I've ever met!

JAMES. *(pacing D. R.)* You're right. Here. *(He crosses L. to her, gives HELEN the play, walks away again, then turns back. Quickly.)* Don't open it yet. Just hold it for a minute. *(They stand looking at each other for a long beat while HELEN holds the play as if weighing it. JAMES is D. R.)* Feel anything? Are you getting any vibes?

HELEN. *(D. C.)* No. I'm not psychic. *(indicating play)* May I?

JAMES. Yes. No. Yes. No. Well... *(two torturous beats, big sigh)* Okay. *(HELEN crosses U. to desk, gets a pair of reading glasses from her purse, crosses to the couch U. C. and sits. She puts her glasses on, takes the play manuscript out of the envelope, then places the script and the envelope beside her on the couch. Next she removes her glasses and examines the lenses carefully.)*

HELEN. *(to JAMES:)* I need my purse. It's in my tote bag. *(JAMES, D. R., crosses U. to the stage R. end of the desk, gets the purse out of the tote bag, and crosses U. above the desk to*

HELEN at couch U. C.) Thank you. *(JAMES crosses back D. R. and continues pacing. HELEN opens the purse, takes a handkerchief out and leisurely cleans her glasses. She puts the glasses on and tosses the handkerchief back in her purse. She places the purse beside her on the couch and picks up the manuscript. A beat. She leans forward, looks at the coffee table, shakes her head, sighs, puts the manuscript back down, picks up her purse and begins sorting through it. HELEN takes the following objects out of her purse and places them next to her on the couch: Her handkerchief, compact, cigarette lighter, Kleenex, keys, scarf, her glass case and a pencil. Disgusted at not finding cigarettes, she throws these items back into her purse, rises, and crosses R. to the desk. HELEN opens the top drawer, rummages around inside it and finally finds a nearly depleted pack of cigarettes. She crosses back to the couch, sits, takes out a cigarette, her last in the pack, crumples the wrapper, and looks for a place to put it. Finally, to JAMES:)* Would you throw this in the waste basket? *(JAMES crosses U. to the couch, takes the crumpled wrapper, hurries to the waste basket underneath the desk, and throws it in. He stands staring intently at HELEN who is finally lit up and ready. She picks up the play. A beat, then to JAMES:)* Oh. The ash tray.

JAMES. *(exploding)* Ahhhggggggggggg!

HELEN. *(sweetly)* On the table. *(indicating)* In the conference room. *(JAMES dashes D. R. into the conference room. After 4 beats, he flies out of the room with half a dozen ash trays, sprints U. C. to HELEN on the couch, places one to her left, one on her right, three on the coffee table in front of her, and one on her lap. HELEN watches JAMES with detatched amusement as he crosses D. L., paces a few steps, then crosses U. to the love seat and plops down. He sits rigidly facing front, eyes squeezed tightly shut, the*

fingers of both hands crossed. After one last whimper from JAMES,
HELEN picks up the play, looks at her shoes, sighs, and opens the
manuscript. There is a long pause. JAMES'S eyes pop open, he
looks U. R. and crosses U. L. A beat, then:)

JAMES. You don't like the title.

HELEN. *(staring at script)* Oh, I think it's quite in-
triguing.

JAMES. *(brightening)* Really?

HELEN. Yes. *(reading)* THE DO IT YOURSELF
BANKRUPTCY GUIDEBOOK. *(to JAMES:)* That's an
interesting title for a play.

JAMES. What? Let me see that! *(JAMES runs U. stage C. to*
HELEN on the couch and snatches the guidebook.)

JAMES. *(leafing through it in panic, on her L.)* Oh, no! Oh,
my God! I don't believe I did this! This isn't my play, I
picked up the wrong envelope! *(holding guidebook at arms*
length) THIS IS MY BANKRUPTCY FILING! *(He drops the*
bankruptcy papers on the couch and storms D. L.) This is
unbelievable! See? See how distracted I am? On THIS
day of ALL days—! *(pounding on his head)* Oh, God! Why
did I DO that? Why did I DO THAT?! You're here,
you're ready to read my play, and I BRING THE
WRONG ENVELOPE!! *(JAMES ends D. R. and continues*
pacing in that area.)

HELEN. *(a beat)* Well. That's that. *(She removes her reading*
glasses, puts them in her glass case and begins putting the items
back into her purse.)

JAMES. *(Stops pacing and whirls to face HELEN.)* What do
you mean?

HELEN. *(rises)* Mr. Skipworth, this changes everything.

JAMES. *(a step U. stage to her)* No it doesn't!

HELEN. *(brightly relieved)* You don't have the play. If you don't have it, I can't read it and holding me here is pointless. So... *(She crosses to the hall door U. L.)* Bring your hammer, pull these nails out and let me go. *(Ends U. stage of door, her left hand on the doorknob, facing stage R.)*

JAMES. *(JAMES is pacing D. R., rubbing his forehead, bouncing on his toes. He sighs loudly, glances at the ceiling for inspiration. He sighs again. Sudden inspiration.)* Ah! *(Runs up to the desk, grabs the phone, and dials)*

HELEN. What are you doing?

JAMES. It's not that far. I'll have Mrs. Heinkle bring it over. *(Paces with receiver to his ear.)*

HELEN. *(two steps toward him)* Now look. There's absolutely no way you can get that play over here in time for me to read it and make my four o'clock appointment!

JAMES. Yes I can. It'll only take ten or fifteen minutes.

HELEN. *(stage L. of JAMES)* Ten of fifteen minutes? *(quick glance at watch)* It's almost three o'clock! I can't read that fast.

JAMES. Just read every other page.

HELEN. *(Eyes to heaven, through clenched teeth.)* I-think-I'm-going-to-EXPLODE! *(As JAMES waits for someone to answer, HELEN mumbles under her breath, steps back to the door, jerks on the knob, gives up, crosses R. to the window on the upstage wall, sees someone in a building across the way and waves her arms wildly. Unsuccessful in getting anyone's attention, she gets the umbrella from the stand in the corner, goes D. to her tote bag on the R. edge of the desk, ties the white handkerchief around the tip of the umbrella, goes back to the window, and waves the umbrella in front of it. After two beats, she gives up, tosses the umbrella back in the stand, crosses L. to the couch and flops down, exhausted. JAMES is still holding the receiver to his ear and pacing below the desk.)*

JAMES. *(to himself:)* C'mon, Mrs. Heinkle, be home, be home. PLEASE be home! *(a beat)* Damn! *(He slams the receiver down, gets another idea.)* Cuff! *(Lifts receiver, dials another number, looks at his watch as he says:)* If he gets here by three ten you'll have forty minutes to read it, you can still make your meeting. *(HELEN glances at JAMES in disgust, then notices his bankruptcy papers on the couch beside her. A take to the papers. She picks them up and studies them as JAMES waits for Cuff to answer.)*

HELEN. You only earned twenty three hundred dollars in the past twelve months?

JAMES. *(still pacing below desk, not looking at HELEN)* What?

HELEN. *(to him:)* I said, you only earned twenty three hundred dollars in the past twelve months?

JAMES. *(Stops D. R. of desk, to her.)* Yes, it was a pretty good year. *(Back to pacing, to himself:)* You've GOT TO be there, Cuff... *(HELEN gets an idea, rises from the couch, goes to her tote bag on the R. edge of the desk, and takes out a can of mace. She hides it behind her back and stalks JAMES during his following phone conversation as he paces D. C. She tries several times to spray him in the face but each time he moves away at the last minute. JAMES speaks into receiver.)* Hello—Cuff? It's Jim— *(He is interrupted.)* What took you so long, I rang ten times. *(not waiting for an answer)* Never mind. Cuff, I've got a real problem, I need you to do something for me right away,

it's very— *(Listens anxiously.)* Just listen, okay? I want you
to go to my apartment, get my play and bring it to me—
(Now D. R., he listens, then shakes head violently.) I can't leave
here! Look, I'll explain when you get here— *(Listens,
moves stage L.)* There isn't any key, Mrs. Heinkle's gone,
you'll have to pick the lock or, I don't know, get in
through the window or something. Cuff, this is VERY
important!! *(Listens, pauses D. L. C., then abruptly changes
directions and goes back toward D. stage R.)* Look, I'm with a
PRODUCER! *(intimately, hoarse whisper)* Helen Osborne...
(Listens, nods.) Yeah, the one on TV, she might produce it,
that's what this is all about. *(Listens, stops D. R., greatly
relieved.)* You WILL? Oh, that's great Cuff, you just saved
my life! Okay. *(Begins crossing to stage L.)* I left it in a manilla
envelope on the dining room table... *(brief pause)* Yeah,
the ironing board, same thing. It's to your right when you
come in. Hop in a cab and come to 111 East 54th Street—
(Listens, stops, facing front, then in disgust:) I'll reimburse you
tomorrow. Will you take a MacDonald's gift certificate?
(Listens, shrugs.) I don't know, Cuff, I think it's for french
fries and a Big Mac... *(Nods, continues D. stage L.)* Yeah, I'm
in her office— *(nods)* Yeah, she's here. Look, Cuff, you'll
have to audition like everybody else! *(HELEN has snuck up
behind JAMES. Now she steps D. stage R. of him and taps him on
the shoulder. He turns to look at her. She holds the can near his face
and depresses the button but nothing comes out. JAMES speaks
into receiver, front.)* —Right, suite 304. Please Cuff—
HURRY! *(He hangs up, crosses below HELEN.)* He's going to
bring it over, it won't be long, just be patient, just be—
*(HELEN tries to spray JAMES as he crosses in front of her, again
with no results. She shakes the can near her ear, then sighs. JAMES*

*goes up to the desk, puts the phone down, then comes back D. stage.
On her R.)* Just relax, try to stay calm... *(Turns to HELEN,
indicating can.)* What's that?

HELEN. *(disgusted)* A can of evaporated mace. *(HELEN
carelessly tosses the can U. over her shoulder. JAMES is off like a
shot. He runs to the window on the back stage wall U. R., glances
out, goes to the double windows R. C., quickly studies the street
below, then hurries to the door U. L., listens, ears against the door,
then drops to the floor and does ten quick pushups. He pops to his
feet instantly and runs easily in place. HELEN has watched
JAMES'S movements with a deadpan stare. She has crossed to U.
C. below the desk. HELEN facing L.)* Can't you slow down to
the speed of light?

JAMES. *(U. L., running in place)* I know, I drive people
crazy. I went to see a clairvoyant once for a reading. She
was very sensitive. She was also obese. I gave her a
headache, she got nasty and said my aura was all screwed
up. *(Stops running in place.)* I told her I'd rather have a
screwed up aura than a big fat one. *(two deep breaths, then to
HELEN:)* She threw me out. I get about two hours sleep a
night. *(He begins doing calesthenics. A new idea occurs to
HELEN. She glances at JAMES, then at the conference room D. R.
and begins edging toward it casually.)*

HELEN. *(moving D. R.)* That's impossible.

JAMES. No, it's not. It's all in your mind.

HELEN. *(lightly)* I a...think I left my lighter in the conference room. *(She ambles casually into the conference room D.
R. JAMES stops exercising and looks after her. A beat. He dashes
D. R. into the conference room. There is the sound of SCUFFLING
off stage.)* Give me that phone you— GIVE IT TO—don't
you—YOU IDIOT! *(A beat. JAMES walks out of the room*

holding an extension phone he's yanked from the wall with part of the wall hanging from it.)

JAMES. *(crossing up to desk)* I'm not going to waste my time sleeping. Besides, I can't sleep until my life is right. Anyway, I don't have a bed. *(He drops the phone extension into the waste basket underneath the desk.)*

HELEN. *(Shoots out of the conference room and strides to the door U. L.)* What do you sleep on?

JAMES. The dining room table. *(above the desk)*

HELEN. *(yanking on the doorknob)* You mean the ironing board.

JAMES. Yeah.

HELEN. *(another yank)* Don't you do anything to relax?

JAMES. Sure. I scream. *(HELEN, intent on getting out, doesn't look at JAMES.)*

HELEN. *(one last yank without results)* Aggghhh! *(Turns, back to door, and surveys the office.)* You scream?

JAMES. *(above desk, sits in desk chair)* It's a voice technique I learned from Cuff. It warms up your vocal cords and releases tension. *(JAMES screams, HELEN jumps, then throws him a disgusted look as she crosses to the window near the bathroom, going above JAMES at the desk.)*

HELEN. What made you decide to become a playwright?

JAMES. *(swiveling side to side in the chair)* I was a writer for Hallmark Greeting Cards. I wanted to make a deeper statement. I quit five years ago. Also I took a playwriting course at Northwestern.

HELEN. *(Arrives at the small up stage window and studies it.)* How have you survived since you quit?

JAMES. Drove a taxi, was a driving instructor, sold shoes. *(He picks HELEN'S Tony off the desk.)* I saw you in *"Candida"* at the Shubert.

HELEN. *(studying the lock on the window)* You did?

JAMES. Yes. You were great.

HELEN. *(Tries to undo the lock. It's stuck.)* I won a Tony for it.

JAMES. I know. Why don't you act on the stage anymore?

HELEN. *(Grabs the window at the bottom and tries to lift it.)* Where have you been? There aren't any good parts for women anymore and the few roles that do come along go to your Elizabeth Ashleys and Sandy Denises. *(HELEN turns front panting.)* Also being...currently on a soap ...doesn't help. People assume...you can't do serious work anymore. *(HELEN reaches behind her with both hands and tries lifting the window in that position.)* I'd love to get a juicy part... *(yanks)* ...but there aren't any... *(yanks)* ...available. *(She stops trying to open the window and leans against it, resting.)* I must have done something to deserve this. *(a beat)* When I was a little girl in Kansas City, I used to kill ants on the sidewalk with a rubber band. Maybe this is my retribution.

JAMES. *(Stops swiveling in the chair and leans forward on the desk.)* You're from Kansas City? I don't believe it! So am I. I went to Southeast High School. Where'd you go?

HELEN. *(crossing D. R.)* I don't care to discuss it. *(Still seated, JAMES pushes himself in the chair around the L. end of the desk, moves D. stage crossing below the desk to the desk's R. end.)*

JAMES. Paseo? Southwest? Northeast?

HELEN. *(Stops D. R., turns to face JAMES.)* I attended the school that had the best Home Ec department in the county.

JAMES. *(still seated, below R. side of desk)* That must have been Central. They were good at everything but sports.

HELEN. *(defensively)* We won the inter-city bake-off my senior year and my cottage cheese pie took first place in the exotic desserts category.

JAMES. Really? *(JAMES rises and crosses D. C.)* You know, it's funny you became a New York producer.

HELEN. Why?

JAMES. *(D. C., L. of HELEN)* Well, you have to be tough and sophisticated to produce here. It seems to me that people from Kansas City are basically naive.

HELEN. Speak for yourself. I've always been tough and sophisticated.

JAMES. Butchering ants is sophisticated?

HELEN. *(crossing L. C. to face him)* I was a little girl!

JAMES. Kansas City, huh? When were you there?

HELEN. Stop being friendly! *(Waves her finger in his face.)* We're enemies, don't you forget that! *(Notices her finger-nail.)* Aggh. Look at that nail—it's broken! You owe me a manicure, Buster!

JAMES. *(shrugs)* Okay. *(Glances at his watch, then crosses above HELEN to the double windows R. C.)* It's been five minutes. Do you think he's got a cab yet?

HELEN. *(Composes herself, then marches L. to the love seat and sits, striking a seductive pose. Low, sultry.)* James?

JAMES. *(looking out windows)* What?

HELEN. This is all unnecessary. Bring your play to my

apartment tonight and leave it with the doorman. I'll read it and call you in the morning. *(JAMES turns and stares at HELEN.)* I'm sure you have talent and if you stick with it, eventually you'll be produced, by me or someone else. Now, I know you're not going to kill yourself, are you, James?

JAMES. *(shyly)* Jim.

HELEN. I know you're not going to kill yourself, are you, Jim?

JAMES. Jimmy.

HELEN. Jimmy.

JAMES. We'll know at five. *(JAMES breaks eye contact and wanders U. R., looking at posters on the walls.)*

HELEN. I don't like the sound of that.

JAMES. *(U. R., studying a poster)* Death is an ugly thing.

HELEN. I happen to think closing before you open is worse.

JAMES. *(over his shoulder, to her:)* I'm sorry about your problem. I have my own problem.

HELEN. *(Still on love seat, she sits up straight.)* Mine is not a problem. It's a crisis! A crisis takes precedence over a problem.

JAMES. *(crossing U. L., behind desk)* Mine is a crisis too. Your crisis is money, mine's life and death. *(Turns to her.)* So mine's bigger.

HELEN. Men! Why do you always have to have a bigger crisis!?

JAMES. *(at U. L. door)* Come on, Cuff, come on—! *(Puts his ear to door, listens.)*

HELEN. Cuff? His name is Cuff?

JAMES. *(to her:)* Link. Cuff Link. Like Rip Torn.

HELEN. *(to him:)* I take it your friend is an actor. *(She is facing stage R.)*

JAMES. *(Steps U. L. C. to photos on back wall, U. of door.)* Yeah, he's pretty good. He got two call backs on Sesame Street last year. *(He stops and stares at one photo in particular, then turns D. to HELEN.)* I didn't know you were a Miss Missouri. *(Turns back to the photograph.)* You look GREAT in a bathing suit. *(He looks at HELEN again as he crosses slowly R. to above desk.)*

HELEN. *(squirming on love seat)* Looked. That was a long time ago. Well, not that long, but...actually beauty is all an illusion, you know...make-up, padding...

JAMES. *(Looks L. at photograph, then back to HELEN.)* Padding? I don't see any padding.

HELEN. *(Faces D., crosses arms covering chest.)* Oh, we women are very clever, it's well concealed...actually, I'm very plain. *(She slumps down.)* If you saw me without this— *(Indicates her clothes, makeup.)* ...you'd be very unimpressed. Very. In fact, I'm not even plain, I'm more like ordinary. *(Slumps more.)* Semi-ordinary. Actually, certain people find me repulsive. *(Makes a face front, then, suddenly cheerful.)* Well! It's time for a cigarette. *(HELEN rises, goes around stage R. end of desk to above desk as JAMES crosses to L. of desk and D. C., watching HELEN as he goes. HELEN begins opening and closing drawers, looking inside. This action continues through the following:)*

JAMES. Do you have to smoke?

HELEN. Yes, I do.

JAMES. *(crossing U. C. to stage L. of HELEN)* When you're breathing deeply like I do, smoke really kills you.

HELEN. *(rummaging through a lower drawer)* I'm sorry. You may be able to keep me here against my will, but you cannot keep me from smoking.

JAMES. Why do you smoke?

HELEN. Because I like it. Why do you pace? *(Slams a drawer, opens another one.)*

JAMES. Because I have all this nervous energy. *(JAMES sits L edge of couch on the arm.)* Anyway, they're not comparable. Pacing won't hurt you but smoking can kill you.

HELEN. Ha! *(Slams drawer, opens another.)*

JAMES. It's true. You probably smoke because you're just as nervous as I am. I'm just more out in the open.

HELEN. You can believe whatever you want. You pace, I'll smoke. Viva la difference!

JAMES. Did you ever go to the Mary Lou Theatre? *(HELEN looks under manuscripts on the desk, behind her Tony.)*

HELEN. I can't be out. I got a carton three days ago. What?

JAMES. The Mary Lou Theatre in Kansas City. Did you ever go there?

HELEN. *(Glances around office with concern.)* No—I don't know. I know I'm not smoking three packs a day, they must be here somewhere.

JAMES. *(off into space, dreamy look)* I used to go there every Friday night and Sunday afternoon just to neck with Marilyn Crow. *(HELEN crosses L above the desk to the couch U. C. She looks at the coffee table, then sees her purse. She grabs it and turns it upside down on the couch. HELEN quickly sifts through the contents, whimpers, suddenly freezes and looks D. R.)*

HELEN. The conference room! *(She dashes D. R. and disappears into the conference room as JAMES rises and takes a few steps in the D. R. direction. A beat. Enter HELEN from the conference room, her face pale.)* I'm out. I'm totally out! *(with growing panic)* Ohmigod! I don't have any cigarettes and I can't get to a drugstore. *(crossing quickly U. C. to JAMES)* You HAVE to let me go. Now! That's all there is to it. I want a cigarette. It is my God given right as a citizen of the United States to smoke and I want to do it RIGHT NOW! *(She is now beside JAMES, stage R. of him.)*

JAMES. Do you know what that stuff does to your teeth?

HELEN. No lectures!

JAMES. You're a beautiful woman. You don't need yellow teeth.

HELEN. *(a step to him)* I'm warning you...

JAMES. Yellow teeth and yellow fingers. What a combination.

HELEN. *(Holds her hands up and looks at her fingers.)* That's nail polish!

JAMES. Yellow nail polish?

HELEN. *(eyes narrowing)* Are you calling me a liar?

JAMES. *(backing up a step stage L.)* You lied about the red wig.

HELEN. That's it! Now you've done it! You're not going to have to commit suicide because I'm going to strangle you with my bare hands, you son-of-a-bitch! *(HELEN lunges for JAMES. JAMES darts D. C. below desk as HELEN recovers and goes D. stage after him. JAMES sprints around the stage R. end of the desk and heads U. with HELEN not far behind.)*

JAMES. *(quickly, over his shoulder)* I have to go to the bathroom. *(He reaches the bathroom door and grabs the doorknob. Then suddenly, remembering the phone, he dashes down to the desk, grabs the phone, runs U. into the bathroom and closes the door barely evading HELEN'S clutching fingers.)*

HELEN. *(pounding on door)* Where are you going? What do you think you're doing? HEY! *(Pounds three times.)* Come out of there, you COWARD! Give me that phone!

JAMES. Oh, no! You're scary. I've seen you get mad on the soap!

HELEN. *(HELEN whirls around, her back against the bathroom door, the look of a caged beast. She does a take to the door U. L., then looks front with glee.)* Now's my chance! *(She runs to her desk, rummages through the top drawer and finds a cork screw. She holds it up.)* Cork screw! *(HELEN runs U. L. to the door and tries to screw a hole through it, gives up, runs back stage R. to the desk and finds a nail file. She holds it up.)* Nail file! Nail file!! Ah ha! *(Glances at door, runs back up to it and tries filing the doorknob off. She gives up and tosses the file to the floor in frustration. HELEN moves around the office searching for a way out. On a sudden impulse, she runs back U. L. to the hall door and pounds on it.)* Help, HELP! Is anyone OUT THERE!? Doesn't anyone WORK on SATURDAYS? *(Listens, ear to door.)* My God, what's this country coming to, we've turned into a bunch of LAZY BUMS! *(crying)* Mr. Sharp? Mr. Sharp in the travel agency! YOO HOO! ROOM 305?! I saw you in there this morning...are you there? CAN-YOU-HEAR-ME?! *(listens)* You can't work half a day, Mr. Sharp, the travel industry needs you! Think of all those poor Americans stranded in Oshkosh! My God Mr. Sharp,

THEY-NEED-TO-GO-SOMEWHERE!

(The PHONE RINGS. HELEN runs stage R. to her desk on impulse looking for the phone. She sees the extension cord and follows it to the bathroom door U. R. C.)

JAMES. *(off stage)* Hello? Who's calling for her? *(a beat)* Hello, Scott, I'm a fan of yours, I loved you in GREEN HELL, you have the wrong number. Goodbye!

(A Loud CLICK as JAMES hangs up.)

HELEN. *(Her face pressed against the bathroom door.)* SCOTT! HELP! I'M BEING HELD BY A PLAYWRIGHT! CALL THE DRAMATISTS GUILD! CALL THE AUTHORS LEAGUE! CALL THE—
JAMES. *(off stage)* I HUNG UP! That was your husband Scott calling from Tijuana.
HELEN. *(pounding on door)* Unlock this door, damn it! Give me that phone!

(The PHONE RINGS again and continues ringing.)

HELEN. Answer that phone! Do you hear me? That could be an emergency call! ANSWER IT!
JAMES. Hello? *(a beat)* No, Mr. Meyer, you have the wrong number...
HELEN. HELP, SIDNEY! CALL THE POLICE, HELP! HELP!!
JAMES. *(off stage)* I HUNG UP!
HELEN. Agggghhhhhhh!

(She turns around with her back to the bathroom door as the phone begins RINGING again.)

JAMES. *(off stage)* Are you calmer now? Can I come out yet? *(A beat as HELEN stands searching the room.)* Mrs. Osborne? YOO HOO! *(pause)* What are you doing?...I'm coming out now...don't forget, I have the hammer... *(beat)* MRS. OSBORNE? *(HELEN begins pacing in front of the desk, thinking. The bathroom DOOR RATTLES.)* It's stuck again.

HELEN. Good! You like it in there? You can just STAY in — ! *(HELEN glances stage L. to JAMES'S briefcase leaning against the wall U. stage of the hall door, runs to it, opens it and takes out some nails. She looks around her office for a heavy object and spots her Tony statue. She goes stage R. to above the desk, grabs the Tony, crosses up to the bathroom door and begins nailing it shut.)* You thought you could outsmart Helen Osborne, huh? You thought I was some naive little pancake from Kansas City, did you? Well, Mr. Smart Guy—! Who's calling the shots now, huh? *(laughing with abandon as JAMES rattles the door)* I'm never going to let you out of there, do you hear me? I'm not even going to report you to the police! I'm going to close up my office and have it FUMIGATED! What do you think of that, you PEST! You PLAYWRIGHT PEST!! *(Starts pounding a second nail in.)*

JAMES. *(off stage)* MRS. OSBORNE? PLEASE!

HELEN. *(laughing through clenched teeth)* Go on, beg! BEG, BEG, BEG, BEG, BEG, BEG, BEG! It won't do you any good! How does it feel being a prisoner now, Mr. Wise Guy?! Huh!? HUH!?? You like it in there, you WORTHLESS WIMP?!! *(singing and pounding:)* DA!

(POUND) DA! *(POUND)* DA! *(POUND)* DA! DA! *(POUND)* DA! DA! *(POUND)* DA! DA! *(POUND)* DA! DA! *(POUND)* DA! *(POUND)*

(HELEN continues pounding gleefully as the Act I Curtain slowly descends.)

END OF ACT I

ACT II

AT RISE: As the LIGHTS come up, HELEN is discovered U. R. at the bathroom door finishing nailing it shut.

HELEN. *(singing, pounding)* DA! *(POUND)*, DA! *(POUND)*, DA DA! *(With three rapid pounds of the hammer she finishes, then steps back to survey her work.)* Beautiful job, Helen, beautiful job!

JAMES. *(off stage)* Mrs. Osborne—? *(Rattles door. HELEN turns D. and goes to her desk. She glances at her watch.)*

HELEN. *(in dismay)* Uggghhh!!! *(She glances around the room quickly.)* Think, Helen, think! *(She hurries up to the small window stage R. of the bathroom door and looks out as she tries to lift the window again with no luck.)* Damn! *(She runs around the R. end of the desk to the double windows stage R. C. and tries to open these windows with no success.)* Thwart, thwart, thwart! *(HELEN goes U. L. to her desk, finds the note she'd written earlier and picks up her Tony statue.)*

JAMES. *(off stage, rattling door)* Mrs. Osborne, please listen to me—

HELEN. *(over her shoulder)* HAH! *(She runs back to the double windows and pounds a hole through the bottom of the D. stage window with the Tony. Then she wraps the note around the award and shoves it through the hole. She looks down at the street below and suddenly crouches by the window. Mouth to the hole.)* That's it, THAT'S IT! Pick it up, PICK IT UP! *(Her body stiffens. She stands up suddenly, her face pressed against the pane*

55

and shouts:) No, no, don't throw it in the trash basket! DON'T—! *(Suddenly crouches again and jams her mouth next to the hole.)* DON'T THROW IT AWAY, YOU IDIOT! IT'S A TONY, IT'S BETTER THAN AN OSCAR!!! *(She rises, faces D. and makes a gesture of futility.)*

JAMES. *(off stage)* What was that noise? Did something break? What are you doing?

HELEN. *(HELEN glances out the double window again and sees a man in a building across the street. Jumping up and down, waving and shouting.)* YOO HOO! HELP, HELP! Mister! MISTER!! HELP, HELP!! *(then, disgusted:)* I'm not playing GAMES! I NEED HELP!!! *(She gives up, gets another idea and rushes to her desk.)* The sketches--! *(She grabs the sketches, leafs quickly through them.)* Four! Good, that's good. Now... *(She glances quickly around the office.)* My purse...lipstick! *(She sees her purse on the couch U. C., crosses above the R. end of the desk and goes up to the couch. She locates her lipstick, then, breathless:)* Okay, okay... *(She crosses back down to the desk, turns the sketches over so the blank side is up, and screws the lipstick out of the tube. There's only a nub left.)* Oh, no! *(She writes an "H" on the back of one of the sketches.)* "H"... *(She turns the next sketch over and makes an "E.")* ..."E"... *(She writes an "L" on the back of the third sketch.)* ..."L"... *(HELEN grabs the last sketch, begins writing the "P" and runs out of lipstick.)* C'mon, c'mon, all I need is a "P," *(HELEN tosses the empty lipstick tube over her shoulder, picks up the sketches, and runs down to the double windows R. C. She leans the three letters on the window sill, facing out, so that to an observer looking at the window from the outside, the letters would read H-E-L. She mumbles.)* Okay, okay...now the "P." How do I make a "P?" *(a beat)* I'll be the "P," I can be a "P!" *(She tries various "P" poses.)* Is that a...does that look like a— *(She stands in front of the window, below the third sketch, facing D., trying to make "P" with her body.)*

(The door to the bathroom rattles and slowly opens. JAMES peeks out enough for us to see the nails sticking thrugh it ineffectively. He watches HELEN'S contortions at the double windows R. C. JAMES crosses to the desk quietly, puts the phone down on the right side of the desk, takes the phone off the hook, then crosses below the desk D. L. He watches HELEN'S efforts to make the letter "P." A beat. She glances over at him.)

HELEN. *(a startled scream)* AH! *(dropping her pose)* How did you get out?

JAMES. If you want to nail a door shut, you have to toe the nails in. *(HELEN looks at the bathroom door. She crosses U. R. near the right end of the door and stares at the nails.)*

HELEN. *(shaking her head)* Just one of those days... *(HELEN shrugs hopelessly, turns D., her body sags and she heaves a loud sigh. She plods heavily D. to the R. end of desk, leans on it with hands and drops her head in despair. She notices the phone receiver is off the hook. Suddenly, her attitude changes. HELEN lifts her head and, still leaning on the desk, looks D. at JAMES. Thoughtfully.)* James. James? You know...I really do understand where you're coming from. The life of a writer is hell. See this poster? *(Indicates a poster behind her on the corner of the wall U. R. JAMES looks U. at it. HELEN turns and crosses U. R. to the poster and surrounding photographs. Then, to JAMES:)* I won't attack you. Come here. *(JAMES, D. stage L., crosses warily up around the L side of the desk, then goes above the desk to U. R. where HELEN is waiting. She indicates a poster on the wall.)* This was a play I produced a few years ago at the Cort. Now this photograph... *(Indicates a photo under the poster.)* ...was taken at Sardi's the night after we opened. The reviews had been vicious and the writer, who'd waited a long time to be produced, like you, was destroyed. *(Looks at JAMES.)* I'd taken him out to dinner to try to console him. *(Looks back at the photograph.)* Unfortunately we ran into one of the drama critics. That's when this was taken.

JAMES. *(left of and below HELEN, peering at the photo)* Which one's the writer?

HELEN. *(pointing)* The one stabbing his fork into the other one. *(JAMES moves in closer R. and studies the photograph. As he does so, HELEN steps back, goes behind JAMES and crosses D. to the R. side of desk.)*

JAMES. I can understand the guy's frustration but I don't like violence. *(JAMES looks D. L at HELEN who is now leaning with her back against the stage R. side of the desk. She instantly assumes an innocent, casual look. JAMES delivers this line to her:)* I was making love to a girl once and she said "hurt me!" I said "whatta ya mean, hurt you?" She was starting to get mad and she said "I like to be hurt!" So I said "Okay, you're short." *(He looks back at the photograph.)* I can't stand hurting people.

HELEN.   Neither can I. *(HELEN grabs the receiver, steps up to JAMES, and bangs him on the head with it. JAMES staggers R. of desk and drops to his knees, holding his head. HELEN darts back to the desk and grabs the phone. JAMES gropes for the phone cord, finds it, and he and HELEN have a tug of war, back and forth three times, JAMES stage R. of her. As they struggle for the phone and receiver, JAMES unscrews the mouthpiece, takes out the speaker element, and screws the mouthpiece back on. [NOTE: If this is too difficult to accomplish during the struggle, JAMES may remove the speaker element while he is in the bathroom.] At length, JAMES wrestles the entire phone from HELEN with a MIGHTY YANK. JAMES is below the desk and HELEN U. L behind it. She grabs a manuscript and heaves it at him.)*

JAMES. *(ducking)* Please, Mrs. Osborne, can't we stop this violence— *(Ducks another manuscript.)* —and behave like two sane, rational human beings? *(On the word "rational" JAMES slames the phone on the desk and on the word "beings" he puts the receiver back.)*

HELEN. NO! *(Throws another manuscript, then two more.)* You've pushed me over the hump, you half-wit! *(Throws another. HELEN glances around desperately for ammunition. She sees the bookcase against the L. C. wall, runs to it, grabs a bunch of paperback plays and begins throwing them at JAMES. JAMES, now below the desk, pulls the hammer out of his belt and bats the books away.)* You want to be a playwright, huh? Okay! I'll introduce you to Elliot Nugent and James Thurber—you MALE ANIMAL! *(Throws play.)* Say hello to George Kaufman—! *(throws)* Moss Hart sends his regards—! *(throws)* Ionesco is simply THRILLED—! *(throws)* Arthur Miller and Tennessee Williams are DELIGHTED—! *(Throws two. JAMES is now D. far R. HELEN picks out a huge, hard cover book from the shelf, whirls and faces him.)*

JAMES. *(backing up)* Not Shakespeare. Not the complete works! *(HELEN smiles wickedly and stalks JAMES who runs U. R. of the R. side of desk in an effort to get into the bathroom, but HELEN goes above desk, beats him to the door and slams it shut. They circle around the desk with JAMES ending up behind it and HELEN stage L. of him. She throws the book, it catches JAMES on the foot.)* OUCH!! *(He drops the hammer, grabs his foot, then hobbles around the R. end of the desk, crosses below it to the love seat and falls onto it. HELEN has picked up the hammer and, now L. of the desk, starts toward JAMES. JAMES looks U. and sees the raised hammer in HELEN'S hand.)* You wouldn't!

HELEN. *(coming D. toward him slowly)* Oh, wouldn't I? Hah! I can see the headline: "PRODUCER/ACTRESS HELEN OSBORNE, VICTIMIZED BY MAD WRITER, GOES BERSERK AND POUNDS HIS FEEBLE BRAIN TO JELLY!" The publicity might even get me some heavy dramatic parts...like LADY MACBETH!

(As HELEN raises the hammer higher and approaches JAMES, the PHONE rings. She backs U. to the desk and answers it.)

HELEN. *(into receiver)* Hello? *(listens)* SIDNEY! *(Relieved, pouring out.)* OH, GOD—! Sidney, am I glad you called! You're not going to believe this, Sid, but I'm being held captive by an insane writer... *(She's interrupted, listens.)* Sidney? Can't you hear me? I can hear you... *(pause)* Hello? Sidney?! *(Looks at receiver, taps it.)* What the hell's wrong with this thing? *(back into receiver)* Sidney? Can't you HEAR ME? *(Pauses, then shouts into the receiver.)* Sid? SID?! DON'T HANG UP, DON'T—! SIDNEY?! *(HELEN jams the button down, gets a dial tone and dials a number as JAMES tries to get up from the love seat. He sits down quickly, not able to put any weight on his foot. HELEN speaks into the receiver.)* Hello, Henri? This is Helen Osborne, I must speak with Sidney Meyer... *(Listens, confused.)* Henri? Hello? Can't you hear me? *(shouts)* I CAN HEAR— *(HELEN suddenly lowers the receiver and looks at JAMES. A pause, then:)* what did you do to this phone?

JAMES. *(on love seat)* I took out the speaker element. *(He holds the element, a round disk, high in the air.)* You can hear the other person but they can't hear you.

(HELEN slams the receiver down and starts D. toward JAMES as the PHONE begins to ring.)

HELEN. Give me that element!
JAMES. *(facing U.)* No.
HELEN. Give me that element or I'll use this hammer.

(The PHONE continues ringing as HELEN raises the hammer. When she is a few feet from him, JAMES pulls a gun out of his coat pocket and points it at his head. HELEN gasps and lowers the hammer.)

HELEN. Oh, my God! Don't do that, please! Put that down.
JAMES. I'll put this down if you'll put that down.

(HELEN backs up and places the hammer on the L end of the desk. The PHONE is still ringing. As she crosses R. to answer it, JAMES limps quickly up to the desk, snatches the hammer as HELEN makes a grab for it, too late.)

HELEN. *(to JAMES:)* You jerk! You rotten, double dealing— *(She snatches up the receiver and yells into it.)* HELLO! CAN YOU HEAR ME? THIS...THIS IDIOT TOOK THE...THE...THING OUT...
JAMES. The element. *(JAMES, now is L of the left side of the*

desk, sticks the hammer in one side of his belt and the gun in the other.)

HELEN. *(Hangs up slowly, then looks trance-like into space.)* That was the operator. I could hear her but she couldn't hear me. *(near tears)* I am so frustrated. I've never been so frustrated in my life. *(She slumps to the floor, her back against the D. stage front of desk, and begins crying.)*

JAMES. *(pacing U. L.)* You don't know how terrible this makes me feel. I don't know myself. If anyone had told me a few weeks ago that today I'd be wrestling a producer and removing her element, I wouldn't have believed it. *(JAMES is now U. L. of desk.)*

(The PHONE rings again. HELEN lets it ring three times, then, still sitting on the floor, reaches back behind her blindly, gropes on the desk, finds the phone and picks up the receiver.)

HELEN. *(to JAMES: still crying)* I just want to see who it is! *(She listens, tosses the receiver over her shoulder, then through sniffles:)* It was Sid calling back. He asked the operator to check the line...so she did...she told him there's nothing wrong...that's why he called again.

JAMES. *(tenderly touching his head)* Do you have any aspirin?

HELEN. *(spitting it out)* In the bathroom!

JAMES. *(crossing D. to below L side of desk, to her:)* Would you get it for me, please? I'm afraid if I go in there, you'll do something drastic. *(HELEN suddenly stops sniffing and fixes JAMES with a deadly stare.)*

HELEN. What can I do that's drastic? The phone doesn't work and you have the weapons.

JAMES. I'm not forcing you to get it. I'm asking you. Please?

HELEN. Oh—! *(HELEN rises and strides into the bathroom crossing U. and around the R. side of the desk. JAMES crosses to the mirror on the L. C. wall U. of the bookcase and examines his wound. HELEN reenters with a glass and two aspirin. She goes D. R. of the desk, then crosses L. JAMES, who has crossed R., meets her C. stage. She gives him the aspirin. He pops a pill in his mouth, swallows it with great difficulty, and quickly sips from the glass of water. HELEN glances at watch.)* It's three thirty!

JAMES. Cuff is coming, be patient. *(He takes the second pill, a quick swig of water and gives the glass back to HELEN. HELEN crosses U. to the desk and puts the glass down.)*

HELEN. Be patient? Oh, GOD! *(JAMES is having trouble swallowing the second pill. He gulps once, freezes, then looks front, eyes wide. He clutches his throat, gasps, turns R., staggers D. and tries to hit himself on the back. He turns and faces U., waves wildly at HELEN, but she ignores him. He stamps on the floor, HELEN, at the desk, turns to him.)* Stop playing games. *(JAMES waves his arms.)* What's the matter with you? *(no answer)* You can't breathe? *(JAMES shakes head "no.")* I should let you choke... *(sudden realization)* You're choking? You're really choking? *(JAMES nods.)* Ohmigod! What do I do?

JAMES. *(hoarse whisper)* Heimlich!

HELEN. What? Who? Heimlich who? *(JAMES steps behind HELEN and shows her the technique. Putting his arms around her waist and holding his fist in her abdomen, he gives a quick jerk in and up. He pantomimes "do this on me." Despite her anger, HELEN steps behind JAMES and uses the technique. They're facing R. The pill pops out into JAMES'S hand but HELEN doesn't know this.)* Can you breathe? Are you all right? *(She is still holding him around the waist.)*

JAMES. *(breathing deeply)* I don't know, I... *(At first relieved, JAMES'S relief turns to desire as he becomes aware of HELEN'S arms around him.)*

HELEN. I think you're better, aren't you?

JAMES. Yeah, I'm...

HELEN. You can breathe, you're relaxing...

JAMES. Yes.

HELEN. Good. *(dropping her hands slightly)* How does this feel?

JAMES. Good.

HELEN. *(dropping hands further)* How about this?

JAMES. A...a... *(HELEN snatches the gun out of JAMES'S belt and points it at him.)*

HELEN. *(on his L.)* All right, Buster—! Give me that element! *(JAMES turns, looks at HELEN, shrugs, then crosses stage R. toward the liquor cabinet.)* Where do you think you're going?

JAMES. Do you have a diet drink?

HELEN. What? I have a gun pointing at you and you're thinking calories? *(JAMES stops, looks back over his shoulder, then casually:)*

JAMES. My mouth is dry. *(He turns and continues R. to the liquor cabinet.)*

HELEN. Hey? Freeze! This is a gun! It could go off. I'm very nervous! *(JAMES keeps walking.)* Okay. This is a warning! *(HELEN points the gun at the ceiling, closes her eyes, and pulls the trigger. The gun clicks. JAMES looks for a soft drink at the liquor cabinet but doesn't see one. He goes U. R. to the desk, pulling a bullet out of his pocket as he goes.)*

JAMES. *(holding up bullet)* I have the bullets and this...

(indicating his head) …is where they're going. *(JAMES, at the desk, picks up the glass of water and is about to take a sip.)*

HELEN. And this is where this is going! *(HELEN dashes for the double windows stage R. JAMES puts the glass down, races D. R. and meets HELEN at the windows before she can throw the gun through the hole she poked out earlier. JAMES grabs it, wrestles it from her, and sticks the gun in his belt. L. of JAMES, punching his chest with her finger.)* You think you're so tough, don't you? Well, let me tell you something. I've survived in this business a long time and I'm a lot tougher than you are. You'd better be on your guard beause I'm going to find a way to get out of here. One false move and you've had it! *(Snaps her fingers in his face defiantly. HELEN crosses U. to the desk chair now below the R. end of desk and sinks into it. JAMES, trying to relax D. R., shakes out his hands, bobs his head from side to side as a sprinter would do before a race, then drops to the floor and does 10 quick push ups. HELEN, staring at him, shakes her head.)* You are without a doubt the purest, the most unadulterated weirdo I've ever known.

JAMES. *(Pops to his feet.)* Yeah, I don't even know myself anymore. I think my personality is disintegrating.

HELEN. Has disintegrated. *(JAMES goes U. C. around the stage L. side of the desk. Now behind HELEN, he picks up the phone cord and begins measuring it out, studying her. During the following, each time she looks back at him, he stops measuring and smiles, then continues when she looks away.)*

JAMES. I want you to know one thing. I'm grateful you didn't let me choke. You're basically a good person. *(still measuring)*

HELEN. Thanks loads. *(JAMES tiptoes R. above the desk, measuring out a long loop of cord and keeping his eyes glued to HELEN.)*

JAMES. You have a few faults.

HELEN. *(looking back at him)* Like what?

JAMES. *(Stops, drops his hands so the desk obstructs HELEN'S view of the cord.)* Well...you're very self-centered... *(letting more cord out)* ...and somewhat narcissistic.

HELEN. *(Turns front, scowls.)* Let's talk about something else, shall we?

JAMES. You asked. *(JAMES has positioned himself behind HELEN. Suddenly he snaps a loop around her waist and arms and begins tying her to the chair.)*

HELEN. Hey! HEY! What's—

JAMES. *(Continues throwing loops around HELEN with the phone cord and tightening them.)* Sorry about this but—

HELEN. *(struggling)* —What are you—for God's sake, STOP IT! Listen to me, you idiot! *(JAMES ties the cord behind HELEN and with a final flourish, stands back and surveys his work.)*

JAMES. Can I get you something? *(HELEN swivels the chair around with her feet until she is facing JAMES, stage R. of her.)*

HELEN. *(Stares at him, then turns front.)* I don't believe this day. I don't believe this life. *(trance-like)* I'm not going to make that meeting. I'm not going to get the money. My show's going to close, my name will be mud...Helen Mud...I'll never be able to produce again. My last two shows were flops... *(JAMES crosses stage R. to the double windows and peers out. HELEN continues tragically, enjoying the pain.)* ...I've got a rotten marriage, Sid is only using me...and now this. My God. Those ants I massacred on the sidewalk in Kansas City really are vindictive. *(HELEN starts to bawl loudly as JAMES crosses behind the desk and goes to the door U. L.)*

JAMES. Well, you always have the soap.

HELEN. No, I don't! The writers have written me into a corner. They've given me a brain tumor. It's incurable! *(sobbing)*

JAMES. I'm sorry to hear that. *(ear to door, listening)*

HELEN. I only have another month to live. *(sniffing)* I'm going into a coma the end of November.

JAMES. *(Crosses D. L. to the love seat.)* Look. They can stretch that out. In a soap, you could linger in a coma for months. Years.

HELEN. My mother's pulling the plug on Labor Day. It's a mercy killing...and I'm the mercy! *(Begins to wail loudly.)*

JAMES. That's terrible. *(Sits on love seat. HELEN struggles to regain control, then suddenly sits up straight.)*

HELEN. I can't stand this. I need a cigarette.

JAMES. There aren't any.

HELEN. Then get one!

JAMES. Just try and forget about it.

HELEN. *(incredulously)* Forget about it? Forget about it?!·

JAMES. *(Leans back in love seat.)* Why do people get so hung up on smoking?

HELEN. *(suddenly tense, HELEN propels the chair L. across the floor to JAMES, then eye to eye:)* You obviously don't have any idea of what it means to be a chain smoker without a chain! When you were without breath a few minutes ago you'd have given anything for air, wouldn't you? Well, that's the way I feel about cigarettes!

JAMES. I'm sorry. I didn't know you were that addicted.

HELEN. *(leaning forward, straining against her cords)* I'M NOT ADDICTED! I can give it up anytime I want to. I just don't want to. Oh, God, I need a cigarette! *(to him:)* Aren't there any butts?

JAMES. *(sitting up)* Mrs. Osborne, the butts are the worst part.

HELEN. *(hoarse, intense)* I don't care! Get one. Find one. If you can't find one, make one!

JAMES. Out of what?

HELEN. Anything! I don't care, I don't CARE! Just make it LOOK like a cigarette! Make it FEEL like a cigarette! *(Makes a motion with her lips. JAMES rises, looks around the office casually, crosses up to the desk with HELEN following him by propelling her chair with tiny steps. JAMES crosses around the R. side of desk and D. R. C. with HELEN right on his ankles, watching him keenly. He looks right, then left, slowly.)* Hurry up! HURRY UP! *(JAMES crosses back U. to the desk, HELEN following. He tears a piece off a manilla envelope, goes back D. C. to the shag rug, tears some fibers out and begins rolling a cigarette. JAMES finishes the makeshift cigarette and sticks it in HELEN'S eager lips. She looks at the cigarette crosseyed, then at him with disgust.)* My lighter's on the desk. *(JAMES gets the lighter, comes back to HELEN, and lights the cigarette.)* Watch my lashes... *(She takes a puff and gags.)* Take it, TAKE IT! *(As HELEN coughs, JAMES takes the cigarette and drops it in the ash tray on the couch.)* Give me a drink! I want a drink and want it right now!

JAMES. Okay, okay. *(JAMES crosses R. to the liquor cabinet, pours a drink, and crosses back to HELEN at C. stage. He lifts the glass to her lips but doesn't give her enough. She indicates for him to tip the glass farther. He does and spills it down her front.)*

HELEN. Ahgggh! Ah, ah, ah!

JAMES. You should have drunk faster. *(JAMES runs to the desk, grabs a Kleenex, hurries back to stage R. of HELEN. He hesitates.)*

HELEN. What are you waiting for? Hurry! HURRY! *(JAMES dabs at HELEN'S chin, neck, and then chest. Suddenly rigid.)* That's far enough, thank you. *(They stare at each other for a beat.)*

JAMES. I've just thought of a way to make all this up to you. *(He circles up around HELEN and goes to the love seat D. L.)* When you produce my play, I'll give you a piece of the writer's percent. *(Sits on love seat.)*

HELEN. How big a piece?

JAMES. Ten percent of my percent.

HELEN. Forget it.

JAMES. Fifteen percent?

HELEN. *(fast, in one breath)* Twenty and that includes your royalties from the Broadway production, all ancillary rights including TV, film, cable, cassette, recordings, electronic reproductions, foreign translations, road companies, stock and amateur, publishing— *(catching herself)* What am I saying? Even if your play is another DEATH OF A SALESMAN, I wouldn't touch it now. *(Turns the chair around so her back is to him.)*

JAMES. *(Glances at watch.)* Where's Cuff? *(Crosses to door U. L.)* He's never going to get here. I know it. Something's happened. This isn't going to work.

HELEN. *(straining against her cords)* You bet it isn't, you just bet it— *(JAMES begins pacing up and down stage L.)*

JAMES. Who am I kidding? Even if he comes, I can't make you produce it. This whole thing's a flop.

HELEN. — a flop, you've got that... *(trying to slip out of the cord)* ...straight, you've got...

JAMES. A stupid, dumb idea...

HELEN. ...stupid...dumb... *(Tries to bite the cord.)*

JAMES. *(Stops D. L., to her:)* Look what I've done, I've kidnapped you, ruined your show...

HELEN. ...stupid...dumb...dumb...

JAMES. I'm not deluding myself another second. *(Takes the gun out of his belt.)* I can't stand any more failure. *(Begins loading gun. As JAMES continues putting bullets in the chamber, HELEN is involved in trying to untie herself. JAMES is D. L., below love seat.)* It's a terrible thing to realize that the high point of your life was necking with Marilyn Crow in the Mary Lou Theatre in Kansas City, Missouri. *(He's loaded three bullets as HELEN looks up and notices.)*

HELEN. JAMES! What are you doing? Put that gun down and listen to me—! You're a good writer, I know it!

JAMES. *(dropping two more bullets in.)* Huh.

HELEN. *(R. C.)* You are, I feel it. *(HELEN propels the chair D. stage.)* Not only that, you're one hell of a cute guy. There's something about you that's very... *(hard to say)* loveable.

JAMES. *(loading another bullet)* I'm shy and masochistic.

HELEN. That doesn't matter, it's what's inside that counts. You have a kind of...Harrison Ford quality... *(JAMES snaps the chamber shut.)*

JAMES. Yeah. Sure. *(Puts gun to temple.)*

HELEN. *(urgently)* Look. If you don't care about yourself, think about me. What if there's a fire, or an earthquake? What if a rat attacks me? New York rats are getting bigger by the second!

(The sound of FOOTSTEPS is heard running down the hall outside.)

CUFF. *(off stage)* JIM? JIM?!
JAMES. Cuff! He made it! It's Cuff!

(More sounds of running as CUFF approaches the U. L. stage door.)

CUFF. *(off stage)* JIM?
JAMES. *(Runs to the U. L. door.)* Cuff. IN HERE! AT THE END OF THE HALL! *(JAMES puts the loaded gun back in his belt as CUFF arrives and begins pounding on the door.)*
CUFF. *(off stage)* JIM? ARE YOU IN THERE? *(HELEN, R. C., shakes her head in disgust. During the following, she continues trying to free herself. She propels the chair up to the desk, looks on top of the desk, moves the chair to the couch U. C., looks at the objects from her purse on the couch, then propels the chair D. R. to the conference room door and tries to Enter it but the chair won't go through. For the remainder of the play, JAMES alternates between playing to CUFF behind the door and to HELEN, tied in the chair.)* Cuff! God, am I glad you got here!
CUFF. *(off stage)* I'm sorry I'm late...
JAMES. —That's okay, do you have— *(nose to the door)*
CUFF. *(off stage)* —I was with my girl friend. I had to leave her at a bad time... *(Rattles the door.)*
JAMES. This is an emergency!

CUFF. *(off stage)* THAT'S WHAT SHE SAID! *(Door rattles again.)*

HELEN. *(whizzing past the desk, mimicking)* "That's what she said!"

JAMES. Do you have the script?

CUFF. *(off stage)* Yeah, I— *(Door rattles.)* —THE DOOR'S STUCK!

JAMES. It's not stuck, it's nailed shut!

CUFF. *(off stage)* WHY IS IT—

JAMES. I DID IT TO KEEP MRS. OSBORNE HERE. SHE'S REALLY BEEN DIFFICULT ABOUT THIS!

HELEN. *(at couch, to JAMES:)* I've been difficult? I'VE been difficult? *(Propels chair L. to JAMES at door.)* You've acted like an animal and you say I've been difficult? You have some gall! I take back every nice thing I said about you. Your quality isn't Harrison Ford, it's Daffy Duck! *(Swivels chair around and goes back to the couch.)*

CUFF. *(off stage)* Is that her, Jim?

JAMES. *(Looks stage R. at HELEN.)* It sure is. *(a beat, then:)*

CUFF. *(off stage, shouting)* HI, MRS. OSBORNE! MY NAME IS CUFF LINK, LIKE RIP TORN? IT'S MY REAL NAME. I SENT YOU A PICTURE SIX MONTHS AGO—!

JAMES. *(to CUFF:)* CUFF!?

CUFF. *(off stage)* I WAS IN *"Spofford"* and *"Father's Day!"* I ALSO PLAYED HAMLET'S FATHER'S GHOST IN SUMMER STOCK!

JAMES. Not now, Cuff!

HELEN. *(as she propels the chair D. R. of the desk toward the conference room.)* I WARN YOU, MR. LINK, ANY FRIEND OF JAMES SKIPWORTH IS AN ENEMY OF MINE!

CUFF. *(off stage)* OH, YEAH? *(a beat)* Well, actually we're not that close.

JAMES. *(Throws hands up in frustration.)* CUFF! KNOCK IT OFF!! *(HELEN arrives at the conference room D. R. The chair becomes wedged in the door frame.)*

CUFF. *(off stage)* Okay, okay, but if the door's nailed shut...

JAMES. I'll pull the nails out, it'll only take a minute... *(JAMES yanks the hammer out of his belt and tries to remove a nail. He does a take to the hammer, then holds it up and sees that it's two-headed.)*

CUFF. *(off stage)* Are you pulling the nails out, Jim?

JAMES. *(at door)* I brought the wrong hammer! *(He drops the hammer, steps back and looks at the bottom of the door.)* See if you can shove it under the door. *(The door rattles.)*

CUFF. *(off stage)* —There's no room—! *(HELEN frees the chair from the conference room door and spins around, facing JAMES U. L.)*

HELEN. James Skipworth, listen to me—

JAMES. *(Stands back from the door and sees the transom.)* Wait a minute! There's a transom... *(Tries transom rod.)* It's stuck. *(JAMES hurries down to the love seat, pulls it back up to the door and climbs up on it. HELEN propels herself slowly U. L. to him.)*

HELEN. *(seductively)* James, if you let me go now, I'll forget this whole incident. I'll pretend I never met you. I won't press charges... *(JAMES tries to open the transom. It's stuck. He pounds on it.)*

JAMES. It's painted over.

HELEN. I may even read your play... *(JAMES continues pounding on the transom until it pops open, leaving a space of an inch at the top.)*

JAMES. *(Puts fingers through space and pulls.)* —There's a crack. *(The transom won't budge.)*

HELEN. *(Stage R. of JAMES)* ...I'll forgive you for every despicable thing you've done today, just let me go. I won't even hold a grudge... *(JAMES stops trying to pry the transom open and jumps down from the love seat.)*

JAMES. *(to CUFF:)* Cuff! It opened a crack. Can you jump up there? Get a page through? *(HELEN, now C. stage, gives up on JAMES and propels the chair toward the double windows stage R.)*

CUFF. *(off stage, strained voice)* I'll try, but when you called, I was in this funny position. When I reached over my girlfriend for the phone, I strained something. *(beat)* I'LL HAVE IT TAKEN CARE OF, MRS. OSBORNE, I CAN STILL ACT!

HELEN. *(at double windows, to herself.)* Get me out of this madhouse! *(JAMES is pacing under the transom, looking up at it.)*

JAMES. CUFF? C'MON!

CUFF. *(off stage)* Okay, okay, I'll try...

(CUFF jumps up behind the door. We see his shadow momentarily through the transom, then he drops out of sight.)

CUFF. *(off stage, moaning)* Oh, no...

JAMES. Cuff? WHAT HAPPENED?

CUFF. *(off stage)* I dropped it! Why didn't you bind it, it came apartment. THE PAGES ARE ALL OVER THE FLOOR!

JAMES. *(facing door)* Find the first page. Get the first page

through, then find the other pages. Hurry!
CUFF. *(off stage, grumbling)* Okay, okay. HERE!

(CUFF jumps up again, we see his shadow for an instant through the transom before he drops from sight. A small slip of paper flutters down. JAMES catches it as the PHONE begins ringing.)

HELEN. *(at double windows, her mouth near hole, shouting)* HELP! HELP!! *(Turns her head to JAMES.)* Answer the phone! SOMEBODY'S CALLING ME! *(Mouth back to hole.)* HELP! HELP!! *(JAMES is facing D., staring at the slip of paper.)*
JAMES. What's this?
CUFF. *(off stage)* The receipt for the cab.

(The PHONE continues ringing.)

HELEN. *(to JAMES:)* JAMES! Did you hear me?
JAMES. *(to HELEN:)* Yes, I— *(Looks back at the receipt.)* Twelve Fifty? Twelve fifty for a cab from 79th and West End to 54th and Park?
CUFF. *(off stage)* There's a parade on Fifth Avenue! Aren't you going to answer the phone? *(HELEN propels herself U. R. of the desk.)*
HELEN. JAMES! I insist! Untie me right now! I demand it! I don't care if you have a gun. I don't care if you shoot yourself! *(JAMES stuffs the receipt in his pocket, goes R. to the desk, takes the receiver off the hook and hangs up.)*
HELEN. DON'T HANG—! You jerk! *(HELEN propels herself over to JAMES and kicks him in the shins.)*
JAMES. Ouch!

CUFF. *(off stage)* HERE'S A PAGE!

(CUFF jumps up, a page comes through the top of the transom and flutters to the floor.)

JAMES. *(Limps U. L, picks up the page and starts back toward HELEN, now C. He glances at the page and stops.)* CUFF? THIS IS THE TITLE PAGE!

CUFF. *(off stage, beat)* Well, give that to her...while I find the first page... *(JAMES crosses below desk to HELEN, puts the page on her lap, then runs back up to the transom.)*

HELEN. *(reading title)* "THE CATFISH COLONEL?" This play is called "THE CATFISH COLONEL?" That's a stupid title! I'm not going to read this! *(She tries to get it off her lap.)*

CUFF. *(off stage)* Here's one and two...

(He jumps up, two pages flutter down.)

JAMES. *(snatching the pages)* I'll read it to you... *(He crosses to C. stage, L of desk.)*

HELEN. *(eyes closed, shaking her head)* I'm not going to listen, I'm not going to listen!

JAMES. *(studying page 1)* Okay. The title of the play is—

HELEN. *(singing loudly)* La, la, la, da, da, da, da—

JAMES. *(to her:)* Mrs. Osborne, will you please stop sing—

HELEN. *(louder)* — LA, DA, DA, DA, DA — *(JAMES crosses below desk to HELEN and shouts in her ear.)*

JAMES. *(reading)* THE CATFISH COLONEL, ACT

ONE, SCENE ONE!

HELEN. *(to JAMES:)* I hate it, I hate it! *(She propels herself D., singing.)* LA, DA, DE, DE, DE—

JAMES. *(He follows her down, shouting:)* It gets better!

CUFF. *(off stage)* MORE PAGES!

(CUFF'S shadow appears behind the transom 3 times and quickly drops out of sight. Each time a page flutters down. The PHONE begins ringing as JAMES sprints U. L. and picks up the pages.)

HELEN. *(loudly, propelling herself D. R.)* DA, DA, DE, DE...

JAMES. *(He has picked up the 3 pages. He stops, clamps his hands to his ears and squints his eyes closed.)* AHHHGGG! *(JAMES sees HELEN'S scarf on the couch, crosses U. C. and grabs it. He goes D. R. to HELEN and gags her with the scarf.)*

HELEN. Hey! What are you DOING!? HEY!! *(muffled by gag)* Hey! That's a designer scarf from Paris!

JAMES. I'm sorry to do this, Mrs. Osborne, but you have to listen. I may only have an hour and five minutes to live!

HELEN. *(through scarf)* — It cost a hundred and seventy five dollars, JERK—! It's a SCARF, NOT DENTAL FLOSS! *(We hear the phrase "Scarf, not dental floss." She stops mumbling, looks at her watch, then continues babbling. While gagged, HELEN'S capitalized words are heard.)*

(CUFF jumps up again, another page comes in.)

CUFF. *(off stage)* JIM? I'LL READ IT WITH YOU, it'll go faster.

JAMES. *(Looks back over his shoulder, to CUFF:)* **WHAT?**

CUFF. *(off stage)* I'll do the play with you...

HELEN. *(unintelligible)* Take this thing out of my MOUTH, for God's sake— *(JAMES crosses U. L. to the door.)*

JAMES. How can you do that? I'll have the script in here.

HELEN. *(unintelligible)* WHO the hell CARES, anyway—

CUFF. *(off stage)* I know it by heart, Jimmy, I've read it enough times with you. I have almost perfect recall. *(shouting)* I'M A FAST STUDY, MRS. OSBORNE. I LEARNED THE PART OF KING LEAR IN THREE DAYS!

JAMES. *(shouting at door)* CUFF? NOW'S NOT THE TIME TO—

CUFF. —I'M ALSO VERSATILE, I CAN PLAY TEENAGERS, OLD MEN...I EVEN PLAYED A DUCK ONCE!

HELEN. *(to CUFF:)* GO PLAY WITH YOURSELF, YOU JERK!

CUFF. *(off stage)* WHAT DID YOU SAY, MRS. OSBORNE? *(HELEN continues mumbling as JAMES comes D. two steps and looks at HELEN.)*

JAMES. SHE CAN'T TALK, CUFF, I PUT A GAG ON HER!

CUFF. *(off stage)* A GAG? LET ME SEE!

(CUFF jumps up several times in quick succession. Each time he lands, he groans.)

JAMES. *(PACES in the stage L. and C. areas as he graphically sets up the opening scene for HELEN using gestures and vocal inflections. He reads the stage directions from the script pages.)* Okay. *(dramatically)* The curtain rises.

HELEN. *(unintelligible)* If you don't untie me, I'm going to THROW UP! *(D. L, she busies herself trying to break free during the following:)*

JAMES. *(reading)* The set: An office in an advertising agency on Madison Avenue, all chrome and silver, very modern, very—

CUFF. *(off stage, owl sounds)* —Hoo, hoo, hoo, hoo hoo...

JAMES. —*(startled, looks up)* ...very chic, very—

CUFF. *(off stage, louder)* —HOO HOO, HOO HOO—!

JAMES. *(Slaps his hand to his head and crosses a few steps U. toward the door.)* Cuff? I changed the opening scene locale. It takes place in NEW YORK CITY, not Louisiana. There aren't any owls in Manhatten!

CUFF. *(off stage)* Oh. Yeah. Okay. *(JAMES turns back D.)*

HELEN. *(unintelligible)* I don't believe this! Where did these JERKS come from?

CUFF. *(off stage)* You using pigeons instead?

JAMES. *(over shoulder, to CUFF:)* No! No pigeons! No owls! The bird sounds are cut! No birds! This isn't about birds! GIVE ME MORE PAGES!

CUFF. *(off stage)* Okay.

(CUFF'S shadow appears behind the transom, then disappears. Two pages flutter down.)

JAMES. *(Goes U., picks up the pages, then turns front.)* Okay. *(reading)* Marvin Platt is discovered. He's at his desk. He's a nice looking man in his 30's with a harried look... *(JAMES continues through HELEN'S mumbling. HELEN stops trying to free herself momentarily and stares at JAMES, panting.)*

HELEN. *(unintelligible)* JAMES! I'm running out of TIME! I've got to GET OUT of here! I've got to— I've got to— *(Takes two deep breaths, then goes back to straining against her cords.)*

JAMES. *(reading, pacing L of desk.)* His intercom buzzes. Marvin pushes the button. We hear his secretary say "Mr. Platt—"

CUFF. *(off stage, interrupts, reading the part of the secretary in a high voice)* —"Mr. Platt? There's a Colonel Brewster here to see you."

HELEN. *(unintelligible)* I'LL KILL him! I'LL kill him DEAD! SKIPWORTH IS CHOPPED MEAT. BEEF RAGOUT—!

(CUFF pops up and down behind transom, another page sails in.)

CUFF. *(off stage)* Does she like it, Jim? WHAT'S HER REACTION?

JAMES. *(pacing, studying page)* I DON'T KNOW, CUFF, STOP INTERRUPTING! *(a beat)*

CUFF. *(off stage, whining)* It's hard being out here, Jimmy, I can't SEE anything. IT'S DRIVING ME CRAZY!

JAMES. *(Stops pacing.)* Cuff? *(quick glance at his watch)* Bear with me. Help me keep this moving, okay?

CUFF. *(off stage, pouting)* All I want is a little understanding.

JAMES. *(exasperated)* Cuff! *(JAMES crosses U. to the door, then:)* Cuff? I do understand. I appreciate you bringing the play over. Thanks a lot. You're a terrific guy, a good friend, and a GREAT actor.

CUFF. *(off stage, a beat)* As good as Olivier?

JAMES. Better.

CUFF. *(off stage)* I am? *(a beat)* Yeah, maybe I am. *(then brightly:)* OKAY, GO AHEAD, JIMMY. OH, HEY! LET ME DO THE PART OF THE COLONEL, OKAY?

JAMES. SURE. *(JAMES walks a few steps D. then:)* Okay. The secretary says... *(reading)* "Mr. Platt, there's a Colonel Brewster here to see you." Marvin says "I don't have time to—" Before he can finish, the door bursts open.

(CUFF makes loud footsteps off stage before he speaks.)

CUFF. *(off stage, as Colonel Brewster)* "Ya have time, I say, ya have time to make a million dollars, don't you, sonny? Hi—! I'm Colonel Brewster Hodgeden and I got a proposition that'll knock yer socks off!" *(HELEN, D. R., begins making gurggling sounds and nodding at JAMES.)*

JAMES. *(Looks up from script to HELEN.)* What are you saying?

CUFF. *(off stage)* "Ah said, 'AH GOT A PROPOSITION THAT'LL KNOCK YER SOCKS OFF!' "

JAMES. *(over shoulder, to CUFF:)* NOT YOU! *(HELEN, eyes wide, seems to be suffocating.)*

HELEN. *(unintelligible)* HELP! HELP! Ugh...ahhh... ohhh...

JAMES. *(to HELEN:)* Be quiet and listen, we're...are you all right? *(HELEN shakes her head no violently and suddenly goes limp, appearing to be unconscious. JAMES runs D. R. to her, crossing between the desk and the love seat, shaking her.)* Mrs. Osborne? *(He removes the gag.)* Mrs. Osborne? Talk to me! *(Pats her face.)* Hello? Oh, God, I've killed her!

CUFF. *(off stage)* YOU GOING TO GIVE ME MY CUE, JIMMY?

HELEN. It's my...heart...have to...lie down...

JAMES. Okay, okay! *(JAMES begins untying HELEN.)*

CUFF. *(off stage, continuing as Colonel Brewster)* "First off, lemme tell ya a little bit about muhself. I was brought up in the bayous of Tennessee where the catfish grow to be eight feet long, that's right, ah said eight feet long. That's a lotta fish, boy! That's more fish'n most folks see in a month a Sundays...orTuesdays or Wednesdays! Know what ah mean, ah said, KNOW WHAT AH MEAN?" *(AS JAMES has been untying HELEN, she has been watching him out of the corner of her eye. Suddenly she grabs the gun and points it at him.)*

HELEN. *(sitting up triumphantly)* I told you I'd win.

JAMES. Mrs. Osborne... *(JAMES backs off going stage L. of HELEN.)*

HELEN. It was a nice try, fella, but you're out of your league! *(HELEN kicks the remaining cord off her legs and body.)*

CUFF. *(off stage, himself)* "Out of your league?" Is that new? Where are we?

JAMES. I thought you were having a heart attack.

HELEN. Of course you did. *(She stands up, pointing the gun at JAMES.)* Heart attacks are easy. *(motioning him toward the phone with the gun)* Now. Put that element back. Hurry! *(JAMES reluctantly goes to the phone on the desk and screws in the element.)* Get over there. *(Indicates stage R. of desk. JAMES crosses stage R. below the desk as HELEN crosses up to the desk.)*

CUFF. *(off stage)* WHAT? Wait a minute! DID YOU REWRITE THIS SCENE, JIMMY?

HELEN. *(at the phone, with derision)* The Catfish Colonel, huh?

CUFF. *(off stage)* Hey, Jim? I'm lost. WHERE ARE WE?

JAMES. *(D. R., to CUFF:)* MRS. OSBORNE HAS THE GUN, CUFF! SHE GOT LOOSE!

CUFF. *(off stage)* She does? She did? Oh... *(a beat, then:)* I TOLD HIM THIS WAS A BAD IDEA, MRS. OSBORNE!

JAMES. *(to HELEN:)* What are you doing?

HELEN. Calling Sid. *(dialing)* Then I'm calling the police. *(She crosses around the L. side of desk to above it.)*

JAMES. Please, don't judge it yet. Let us do some more.

HELEN. I've heard more than enough, thank you.

CUFF. *(off stage)* MRS. OSBORNE?

HELEN. *(to JAMES:)* You're in big trouble, young man. *(above desk, holding receiver to ear and keeping gun trained on JAMES)*

CUFF. *(off stage)* MRS. OSBORNE?

HELEN. *(over shoulder, to CUFF with irritation:)* WHAT?

CUFF. *(off stage)* How did you like my interpretation of the Colonel?

HELEN. *(over shoulder)* IT WAS INCREDIBLE!

CUFF. *(off stage)* It was? You really liked it? That's great!

JAMES. Mrs. Osborne, you said you were looking for a great part. This is it!

HELEN. *(into phone, urgently)* Don't put me on hold, don't— *(they do)* DAMN! *(to JAMES:)* What are you talking about?

JAMES. *(R. of desk, desperately)* The part of the Colonel, it's a great starring role!

HELEN. *(laughing, to him:)* You're insane

JAMES. Mrs. Osborne, the Catfish Colonel is a woman!

HELEN. *(into receiver, turning front)* Yes, would you page Sidney Meyer, please? *(to JAMES:)* What?

JAMES. *(great intensity)* Colonel Brewster is a woman, Stephanie Morris! Look. We start with her at a point of crisis. She wants to open a chain of fish restaurants but no one will take her seriously because she's a woman. So, she's disguised herself as the Catfish Colonel. *(a step to HELEN)* She's sharp, she's attractive, she's got charisma! This is a play about identity crisis, about role playing. *(HELEN has gotten pulled into JAMES'S pitch against her better judgement.)*

HELEN. *(still on phone)* It'll never work.

JAMES. Sure it will! Look at SOME LIKE IT HOT, TOOTSIE, YENTL! You'd be a smash in the part, I know you would, this could put you on top!

CUFF. *(off stage)* DID YOU THINK MY SOUTHERN ACCENT WAS AUTHENTIC?

HELEN. *(into receiver)* What? *(Listens, then:)* No, no, no—! He's there, he's at a table in the rear. *(listens)* Thank you. *(She begins pacing anxiously.)*

CUFF. *(off stage)* I can do a lot of accents, Mrs. Osborne:

(Chinese accent:) AH, FAVOLET SON, I AM HOPPY TO SAY, CHARLIE CHAN HAS SOLVED MURDER...

JAMES. Think of the acting possibilities! A woman playing a man! You're one of the few actresses alive who could bring it off. *(pointing to imaginary marquee:)* HELEN OSBORNE IN "THE CATFISH COLONEL!" You'd be great!

CUFF. *(off stage, continuing Chinese accent, laying it out broadly, rolling his r's)* COUNTESS DID IT IN RIVING ROOM WIV ROPE! AH SO! AH SO!

HELEN. *(into receiver)* Hello, Sidney, it's me... *(She is interrupted, becomes rigid, then defensively:)* I've been... detained... *(Listens, shakes head.)* I wasn't able to answer the phone. *(Listens, then looks at watch.)* Yes, I know what time it is, something happened to me that...

CUFF. *(off stage, German accent)* LIE DOWN ON ZIS COUCH VIT ME, MRS. JONES, UND I VILL PSYCHOANALYZE YOUR LIPSSSS! AH, AH, AH!

HELEN. *(Listens, her expression changes to anger.)* Well, couldn't you stop him? You must have known I'd have been there if I could, you know how much this meeting meant to me!

CUFF. *(off stage)* THAT WAS GERMAN!

HELEN. *(Listens, then with voice rising:)* —Sidney! Something extraordinary happened! *(listens)* Well, if you'd be still and listen, I'll tell you— *(Listens, begins pacing above desk.)*

CUFF. *(off stage, Irish accent)* Listen, me bie, a little bit of the bubbly never hurt anyone, never did, no, no, never did...

HELEN. —Well, I'm sorry I made YOU look bad! *(lis-*

tens) Stop shouting, Sidney! *(listens)* Sidney, listen to—I—*(shouting)* HEY! I'VE JUST BEEN THROUGH HELL AND I DON'T NEED THIS! GOODBYE! *(HELEN slams the receiver down. She stands paralyzed for a moment, then walks deliberately to the couch U. C. and sits rigidly. She stares front, numb.)*

JAMES. *(a beat)* You missed your meeting, didn't you? *(HELEN looks at JAMES blankly.)* I'm sorry. I feel terrible. Look, you'll have another chance to see Fowler or someone else.

HELEN. *(stoically, staring front)* I don't know anyone else.

JAMES. *(above desk)* Maybe you could—

HELEN. *(dramatically)* —It's all over. That's it. I not only lost my investor, Sidney walked out on me. You should have heard the way he talked to me.

JAMES. I'm sorry, Mrs. Osborne.

HELEN. I'm not surprised. My break up with Sid's been coming for a long time. I'm glad it's over...and I don't have any delusions about Fowler. He'd have wanted everything—

CUFF. *(off stage)* I do my own make up, Mrs. Osborne, I have my own wardrobe. I WORK CHEAP!

HELEN. *(to JAMES:)* I was desperate, he knew I was desperate, people take advantage of you when you're desperate.

CUFF. *(off stage)* MORE PAGES!!

(He jumps up, more pages flutter in.)

HELEN. *(loving the misery)* I'm up to my eyeballs in debt.

Scott got drunk two years ago and drove the car up the steps of the 42nd Street Library. He ran over an Armenian selling pretzels. I'm still paying the lawyers—! *(She starts to sob loudly. JAMES goes tentatively to U. R. end of couch.)*

JAMES. That's terrible.

CUFF. *(off stage)* What's happening? WHO'S CRYING?

JAMES. *(to CUFF:)* Mrs. Osborne!

HELEN. *(still holding gun)* And now Scott's leaving me. He's leaving me for an ingenue! My God, she has freckles! An ingenue with freckles! He met her in a touring company of "The Fantasticks"...

CUFF. *(off stage)* You know, I have this uncanny ability to cry at anytime—REAL TEARS—!

JAMES. *(sits on R. edge of couch)* I'm sorry.

HELEN. He's 30 years older than she is. She's only 22, she's a child! *(to JAMES:)* How do you compete with children? *(Looks front.)* Not that I'm that much older than she is...

JAMES. *(scooting closer to her)* You don't look any more than 30, Mrs. Osborne.

HELEN. *(comforted, to him:)* 30? You really think so?

JAMES. *(moving closer to her)* Not a day more. *(CUFF begins crying off stage as HELEN continues.)*

HELEN. But I don't have freckles. Do you see any freckles on this face? Anywhere on this body? *(JAMES has been inching L. toward HELEN on the couch. Now he is beside her.)*

JAMES. *(studying her face)* No, I don't. But I'm not a freckle man.

HELEN. *(to JAMES:)* That's why I've been seeing Sidney, I had to prove to myself I still had some value, some worth. *(She looks front and begins to sob again.)*   I HATE MYSELF!

JAMES. *(Puts his arm around her.)* Look, I know— *(CUFF begins sobbing loudly off stage with HELEN. HELEN continues crying for a beat, then tires of competing with CUFF. She sits upright on the couch, pushing JAMES off. JAMES falls to the floor.)*

HELEN. I'm going to end this farce! I'll jump out the window, I'll— *(noticing the gun in her hand)* Ah ha! *(HELEN holds the gun up as CUFF stops sobbing.)*

JAMES. *(getting to his feet, R. of HELEN)* You don't want to do that, Mrs. Osborne, that's not the answer.

HELEN. It was for you. You were going to end it all if you weren't successful, weren't you?

JAMES. *(to above desk)* I thought I'd try. I don't know if I could...

CUFF. *(off stage, sniffing loudly)* I NEED A KLEENEX!

HELEN. *(D. R., facing L)* Well, I know I can. I've got the reason, the determination... *(Holds gun up.)* ...and the means. *(She slowly puts the gun to her head.)*

JAMES. *(blurting, in one breath)* Mrs. Osborne, wait! This isn't going to help! You can't see it now but in a little while it won't be as black as it seems, I know it. You'll wake up tomorrow and feel a lot better—!

HELEN. *(dramatically)* There won't be any tomorrow, James. Not for the late Helen Osborne.

CUFF. *(off stage)* Oh, here's one in my back pocket.

JAMES. Look... *(Starts toward her around L. of desk.)* Just...let's talk for a few minutes, okay? *(HELEN points a finger at JAMES.)*

HELEN. Stay where you are!

JAMES. *(Freezes D. L. of desk.)* If you have to shoot somebody, shoot me. I caused this.

HELEN. *(incensed, lowering gun)* I'm not going to shoot you! I'm not a murderess.

JAMES. You will be if you shoot yourself.

CUFF. *(off stage)* HEY? WHAT'S GOING ON?

HELEN. Suicide is not murder. It's suicide!

JAMES. It's the same thing.

HELEN. It is not! Suicide is NOT a synonym for murder!

JAMES. Yes it is!

HELEN. *(furious, pointing L. to bookcase)* Show me in the dictionary! Webster's New 20th Century, Unabridged, Second Edition!

JAMES. Well, I—

HELEN. Ha! See? You know I'm right!

CUFF. *(off stage)* DON'T DO IT, MRS. OSBORNE, DON'T SHOOT YOURSELF! YOU'RE THE ONLY PRODUCER I KNOW—! (Cuff begins jumping up repeatedly.)

JAMES. *(a step to her)* Okay, then, I'll tell you what. If you won't shoot me, let me kill myself first. You can do it second. I couldn't live knowing I was responsible for your death.

HELEN. That's your problem. *(gun to head)*

CUFF. *(off stage)* I know a little bit about psychology, Mrs. Osborne. I took Psych I at NYU in summer school. Maybe I can help.

HELEN. *(D. R.)* HAH!

CUFF. *(off stage, pendantically)* You know, I learned that most suicides kill themselves around Christmas when it's cold and they're lonely and sad and don't have anybody to love them and they just feel totally depressed and hopeless... *(HELEN has gotten progressively depressed by CUFF'S "help." She lowers the gun and sobs loudly. A beat, then brightly:)* So what I'm saying is, now's a terrible time to kill yourself. You should wait a few months!

HELEN. That does it.

JAMES. *(over shoulder to CUFF:)* CUFF! YOU'RE NOT HELPING!

CUFF. *(off stage)* I'm not? *(a beat)* MORE PAGES!

(CUFF jumps up, more pages flutter in.)

HELEN. I can't stand it another second.

(She raises the gun to her head as JAMES sprints D. R. to her and grabs the gun. They wrestle for control of the weapon. It should be held high, over their heads at arms length. JAMES yanks it toward him, HELEN yanks it back. They repeat this process. On the third yank, the GUN goes off three times. Instantly a bottle breaks on the liquor cabinet, two posters fall off the walls, and the transom drops open. HELEN staggers to the couch and drops on it panting. JAMES goes to the love seat L. C. and sits facing R. holding the gun. Although the transom has dropped open, we still don't see CUFF.)

CUFF. *(off stage)* Did someone just try to shoot me?

HELEN. *(Collapses on the couch, face down, kicking and pounding with her fists.)* I want to die! I want to die! I want to die! Why did you stop me, why, why, why?

JAMES. *(rising from love seat)* I know you feel badly, Mrs. Osborne, but let's... *(picking up and sorting pages)*... read a scene, it'll get your mind off of everything... *(He crosses U. L. to the door and picks up the remaining pages, then crosses U. R. to HELEN and sits on the L. edge of the couch.)* Now remember, this play is about the plight of contemporary women and—

HELEN. *(Bats the pages away.)* I hate this play! I'll never do it, never! My life is ruined. It's over. *(HELEN continues moaning on the couch, pounding and kicking.)*

JAMES. So is mine.

(JAMES sighs, looks at the gun in his hand, gets up and crosses D. L. as CUFF'S head appears at the open transom. He's outside, standing on a chair.)

CUFF. Hi, Mrs. Osborne. *(big smile)* It's me. Cuff.

JAMES. *(body sags, forlorn look)* I can't go back to my apartment, to baloney sandwiches on day-old-bread...

CUFF. *(brightly, looking D. at JAMES)* Hi, ya, Jimmy! How's it going?

JAMES. —To droopy shorts with no elastic— *(CUFF sticks his head through the transom opening and looks around the office.)*

CUFF. Boy, I feel a lot better now that I can see everybody! This is a swell office, Mrs. Osborne.

(The PHONE rings.)

HELEN. *(big sigh)* Oh, God! James? I don't want to talk to anybody.

(The PHONE continues ringing. JAMES is undecided whether to shoot himself or answer the phone. He decides on the phone and crosses U. to the desk.)

CUFF. *(to HELEN:)* How'd you like my accents, Mrs. Osborne? You know, I was crying real tears out here. I have the Kleenex to prove it! *(Holds up a bedraggled tissue.)*

JAMES. *(answering phone)* Hello? *(Listens, nods.)* Yes, she's here but— *(Hand over receiver, to HELEN:)* It's Scott.

HELEN. *(drying her eyes)* I can't talk to him now.

JAMES. *(into receiver)* She can't talk now, she just— *(He's interrupted, listens, then to HELEN:)* He says it's urgent. *(HELEN sighs, rises, crosses D. to the desk and takes the phone from JAMES. JAMES crosses D. L., his shoulders slumped, his face drawn.)*

HELEN. *(into receiver)* Hello? *(listens)*

CUFF. *(to HELEN, brightly:)* I have a good face, don't you think, Mrs. Osborne? They say I'm photogenic. *(He strikes a head pose.)*

HELEN. *(into receiver)* A divorce? *(Listens, nods.)* No, I agree, with you, Scott. It is time to legalize your position. How far along is she?

JAMES. *(to himself, trying to get his courage up)* Okay, James. This is you moment of truth. *(gun to head)*

HELEN. *(on phone)* That far.

CUFF. *(reaching in with script)* Here, Jimmy. Here's the rest of the script.

JAMES. *(still holding front, tragically)* I won't be needing it now.

CUFF. Oh. *(Looks at HELEN.)* Well, maybe when Mrs.

Osborne gets off the phone, we can finish reading it to her.

JAMES. *(shaking head)* I don't think so.

HELEN. *(into receiver, false gaiety)* No, Scott, really, I'm relieved. I've been wanting to tell you for months...I've met someone. *(Looks D. L. at JAMES.)* —A playwright— *(nods)* —a few months ago...

CUFF. *(to HELEN:)* Everybody says I'm a good type. What do you think?

JAMES. *(to himself:)* Okay, Jimbo. It's now or never.

HELEN. *(Nods, into receiver.)* Yes. *(Looks at JAMES.)* He's very special, very talented and handsome. And he's written a play for me.

JAMES. *(facing D. L.)* I can't do it. *(Lowers gun.)* I'm not sick enough.

CUFF. *(cheerfully)* I'm five two, Mrs. Osborne, but I have lifts.

HELEN. *(on phone)* —It's about a woman in crisis. I play a woman playing a man. It'll be another TOOTSIE, another YENTL!

JAMES. Suicide is the coward's way. I'm not a coward.

CUFF. *(to HELEN and JAMES:)* My whole family is short, including my uncles and aunts—

HELEN. *(on phone, laughs)* No, Scott, this part was written for a real woman, not an ingenue with freckles!

JAMES. —Then again, I'm probably going to prison so I might as well do it. *(gun to head)*

CUFF. —My Uncle Bobbie is only five one, but he doesn't care. He has over a hundred oil wells.

HELEN. *(on phone)* Good luck, Scott. You'll be hearing

from my attorney. *(Hangs up, stands staring into space.)*

CUFF. I have a picture and resume with me, Mrs. Osborne. *(He disappears, then reappears with a picture which he holds up next to his face.)*

JAMES. *(Lowers gun, brightly)* I can write in prison...and I'll be living rent free!

CUFF. I'll just drop it in... *(He drops the picture and resume into the office. HELEN is pacing U. C. Suddenly she stops, facing front.)*

HELEN. Did someone— *(Points with a sharp movement at CUFF while looking front.)* —mention something about— oil wells? *(She does a slow take to CUFF at transom.)*

CUFF. Yep. Uncle Bobby's one of the richest men in the Panhandle. *(HELEN crosses to the transom and stares up at CUFF.)*

HELEN. You ARE a good type! Give me the script. *(CUFF hands the remaining pages to her. She crosses C. stage, studying pages.)* James? You said she's educated? Bright and sexy? *(looking at JAMES.)* James?!

JAMES. What?

HELEN. *(HELEN crosses around R. side of desk, U. R.)* You said Stephanie is bright and sexy?

JAMES. *(Turns to her.)* Yes. Why?

HELEN. How many characters?

JAMES. Ten. Two starring parts—

HELEN. *(getting an idea)* Uh, huh...uh, huh...How many sets?

JAMES. It's fluid. Sets are suggested, we create the atmosphere with lighting.

HELEN. *(nodding)* Uh, huh... *(studying pages)* Read this with me. *(She crosses D. to JAMES and points to a page.)*

JAMES. Why?

HELEN. Do it! Here. *(She holds pages so JAMES can see.)*

JAMES. I know it by heart. *(JAMES crosses R. above HELEN.)*

CUFF. *(excited)* Hey? Can I read, too?

HELEN. *(to CUFF:)* No, Mr. Link, I need your critical eye on my performance. All right?

CUFF. *(humbly)* I'm honored.

HELEN. *(R. of JAMES)* All right. From page 97, the last scene. *(looking at script, reading)* The board members exit in defeat. Marvin and Stephanie are left alone standing at opposite ends of the long conference table.

JAMES. *(as Marvin)* "You're the best damn negotiator I've ever seen."

HELEN. *(as Stephanie)* "How do you feel about that?"

JAMES. "I can live with it. I like strong women."

HELEN. "Most men don't."

JAMES. "That's their problem."

HELEN. *(slowly crossing R. to JAMES)* "No, it's not. It's my problem. I've always been bright, strong willed, opinionated...and I'm a nice person. In college I was Phi Beta Kappa and Home Coming Queen and I had three dates in four years. What does that tell you, Marvin?"

JAMES. "That you went to school with a lot of dumb guys."

HELEN. *(laughing)* "Marvin? Have you ever been kissed by a Colonel?"

JAMES. "Not that I know of." *(HELEN lifts JAMES'S head and kisses him gently. The kiss becomes passionate.)*

HELEN. *(recovering, clearing her throat)* Not bad for a

writer. *(Walks a few steps away from JAMES, studying pages.)* I don't see this as a play at all.

JAMES. *(panting, L. of her)* I know that...

HELEN. — But I think it would make one hell of a good musical! *(Looks at JAMES.)*

JAMES. What?

CUFF. *(jumping up and down)* Great idea, Mrs. Osborne, GREAT IDEA!

HELEN. *(sweetly, to CUFF)* Do you think so, Mr. Link?

CUFF. Yes! Call me Cuff.

HELEN. Cuff. *(looking at script, pacing in D. R. area)* I like her, I really like this woman! I think it can make a great concept musical like *"Dream Girls"* or *"Chorus Line."*

CUFF. *(eagerly leaning into the room)* I don't know if Jimmy told you, Mrs. Osborne, but I'm a wonderful singer.

JAMES. *(L. C.)* Mrs. Osborne, does this mean you're interested in producing my play...as a musical?

HELEN. Yes. It lends itself perfectly to the musical idiom.

JAMES. You mean you're not going to have me arrested?

HELEN. *(Stops R. C.)* Of course not, James, why would I do a thing like that?

CUFF. I'm a lyric baritone.... *(HELEN turns and goes R. to R. D. area.)*

HELEN. The more I think about this, the more I like it! I've always wanted to do a musical.

JAMES. *(evasively, sitting on love seat)* I don't know anything about musicals.

HELEN. *(studying pages)* Don't worry, James, we'll get the top creative people to do the score and lyrics. You'll be with the pro's, you'll write it together.

JAMES. *(half-heartedly)* Great. We'd...have to totally rewrite it?

HELEN. *(Turns and faces JAMES.)* Of course, but we'd keep the essence of it, maybe lighten it, fluff it up...

JAMES. Oh.

HELEN. James, it can work, I know it can. *(to CUFF:)* Don't you agree, Mr. Link?

CUFF. Yeah. Right. Absolutely! Oh, by the way, I have a two octave range, maybe two and a half!

JAMES. *(pondering the idea)* Great. Yeah...it might work, but...this is supposed to be a serious study of human sexuality.

HELEN. *(Crosses to R. of JAMES.)* That's perfet. That makes it contemporary.

JAMES. *(Rises and begins pacing L. C.)* A musical, huh? Well. I don't know, I...I'm having trouble seeing it that way.

HELEN. *(Turns her back to him, faces stage R.)* You'll get used to it. *(studying pages)*

JAMES. Well maybe...but, look. I don't want to seem ungrateful, I'm glad you're interested in my play, I mean, that's why I went through all this, but I think... *(R. C., he turns to face her.)* ...a musical might take away the bite.

HELEN. *(facing him)* No it wouldn't, it would enhance your material, I know what I'm—

CUFF. —Low A flat to high A flat—

JAMES. *(L. of love seat)* Well... I really don't think so. Why not do it as a play first and then—

HELEN. *(laying it out)* —James, listen to me. I'm a producer. I guarantee this has a real chance as a musical but not as a play.

JAMES. Why not?

HELEN. People don't want to see plays unless they're brought over from England. We can make this a splashy musical, throw in a lot of special effects, have dancing catfish, singing french fries—and at the end, Marvin and the Colonel can fly off together on a giant, revolving cherry pie!

CUFF. WOW! oh, WOW!

JAMES. *(a sickly look)* I don't think it would—

HELEN. *(pacing, excited)* I'm taking this to the Shuberts!

JAMES. Mrs. Osborne, I do't see my play as a musical.

HELEN. *(two steps to him)* It's either a musical or zilch! *(They stand glaring at each other with the love seat between them. Then JAMES makes a decision. He takes the pages from HELEN, picks up the hammer, crosses U. to CUFF at the transom and gives the hammer to him.)*

JAMES. Cuff, would you please knock the nails out for me?

CUFF. *(taking hammer)* Sure. *(Hesitates, looks at HELEN.)* Is it okay with you, Mrs. Osborne?

HELEN. *(to JAMES:)* What are you doing?

JAMES. *(Turns and crosses to desk, picking up pages of his script.)* I'm leaving, Mrs. Osborne. I hope you can forgive me for all this. I'm sorry I—

HELEN. *(incredulous)* You're LEAVING?!

JAMES. Yes.

HELEN. After all you've put me through? Fat chance! *(HELEN pushes the desk chair against the back of JAMES'S legs causing him to fall backward into it. HELEN quickly grabs the phone cord and ties JAMES to the chair.)*

JAMES. What are you doing?

HELEN. *(with maniacal glee)* You are a fruit cake, you know that? After all you've done today, you're going to just walk out that door? You're going to walk away from an offer of a PRODUCTION?! Just because I want to do it as a MUSICAL?! I was right all along. YOU ARE CRAZY!

JAMES. But—

HELEN. *(Finishes tying JAMES to chair, L. C.)* Listen to me, James Skipworth. Do you know what this could do for your career? Do you know how much money you could make? Five thousand a week, minimum!

CUFF. Five thousand? Dollars?

HELEN. *(to CUFF:)* At least! *(to JAMES:)* Not to mention other companies and the film sale!

JAMES. But I just can't see it, Mrs. Osborne

HELEN. You can't see it? YOU CAN'T SEE IT? You're blind, fella.

CUFF. *(in awe, picturing it)* I can see it, I can see it!

HELEN. *(to JAMES:)* I'll draw you a picture. *(HELEN runs to the closet D. L, opens the door, and disappears inside. Objects come sailing out: an umbrella, several coats, some hats, ear muffs, a broom, dust mop, and a music stand.)* This play has every ingredient for a hit musical. We can open it up, razzle dazzle 'em. With me in it, this can be a smash! *(A beat. HELEN Enters from the closet playing the accordion haltingly.)* I'm a little stiff—

JAMES. You play the accordion?

HELEN. *(shouting over sound)* MY MOTHER THOUGHT IT WOULD HELP DEVELOP MY BREASTS. GOD, WAS SHE RIGHT! (HELEN plays a riff.)

CUFF. Wow! What talent, what talent!

HELEN. I'm made for that part, James, made for it!

JAMES. I'm not sure about this...

HELEN. *(playing chords)* You will be when I get through with you!

CUFF. I'd like to sing for you sometime, Mrs. Osborne...

HELEN. *(C.stage)* How do you like them apples, huh? Eat your heart out, Lawrence Welk!

CUFF. *(looking around the office)* Do you have a piano in there?

JAMES. *(Clears throat.)* Five thousand a week?

HELEN. Minimum, BARE MINIMUM! *(to CUFF: shouting over accordion)* I'D LIKE TO MEET YOUR UNCLE SOMETIME, MR. LINK!

CUFF. He's flying up next week in the Lear.

HELEN. SET IT UP. I LOVE SHORT GUYS!

CUFF. Okay. HEY? MAYBE I COULD SING A FEW BARS FOR YOU NOW! CAN YOU SEE MY FACE OKAY?

HELEN. *(HELEN hits a chord.)* HIT IT!

CUFF. *(hitting a high note)* AHHHHHHHHHHHH!!! *(The chair he's standing on gives way, CUFF falls out of sight.)* HELP!

JAMES. *(looking front)* Helen Osborne in THE CATFISH COLONEL by James Skipworth...*(beat)* Well...

(HELEN continues playing arpeggios as CUFF breaks through the door and joins in singing scales to HELEN'S accompaniment, Dancing and "selling" himself as...the CURTAIN FALLS.)

THE END

FURNITURE AND PROPERTY PLOT

On Desk Right Center
    Box of Kleenex
    Equity contract
    Limited Partnership offering
    Equity Rule Book
    Purse
    Unopened manilla envelopes containing play
      manuscripts
    Tony statue
    Rotary telephone with 20 to 25 foot cord
    A stack of 8X10 glossies with resumes

Inside Desk Top Drawer
    Corkscrew
    Pack of cigarettes containing 1 cigarette
    Nail file

Inside Desk Side Drawer
    Doll with large pins sticking through it

Under Desk
    Waste paper basket

On Couch Up Center
    8 brightly colored pillows

On Floor Up Right Corner
    Umbrella stand with umbrella inside

Left Center
     Backless circular love seat

Off Up Left by Hall Door Leading to Outside Hall
     A chair

Off Down Right in Conference Room
     6 ash trays
     4 set sketches (at least 24 by 30 inches)
     A phone with a section of wall hanging from the
        cord

On Liquor Cabinet Down Right
     4 bottles of liquor, 1 opened with plastic cap,   half
     full
     3 glasses
     1 shot glass

In Bathroom Up Right
     1 glass
     2 aspirin

Coffee Table Below Couch

In Closet Down Left
     Umbrella
     2 coats
     3 hats
     Pair of ear muffs
     Broom
     Dust bin

Mop
Music stand
Pair of boots
Accordion

Down Center
    Woven throw rug

Behind Desk Right Center
    Chair on casters without arm rests

Bookcase Left Center
    Paperbacks of plays
    1 hardcover copy of Shakespeare's Complete
    Plays

Over Bookcase On Wall
    Posters of past productions
    1 mask of tragedy
    1 mask of comedy

On Wall Upstage Of Bookcase
    1 mirror

On Wall Up Left
    4 photographs of Helen Osborne in bathing suit

Up Right On Wall Upstage of Double Windows
    1 poster
    1 photograph beneath poster

PERSONALS

HELEN OSBORNE
Hat pin
Hat with red wig attached
Purse containing:
 Handkerchief
 Compact
 Cigarette lighter
 1 Kleenex
 Keys
 Reading glasses in case
 Lipstick
Tote bag containing:
 Scarf
 A can of Mace (empty)
Wristwatch

JAMES SKIPWORTH
Briefcase containing:
 Bankruptcy papers in manilla envelope
 8 nails (4 inch)
 Two-headed hammer
A revolver
6 bullets
Pen
Several sheets of toilet paper (used as Kleenex)

CUFF LINK
Pages of a complete play manuscript (unbound)
Picture and resume
Wristwatch
Receipt for cab

SOUND PLOT

Toilet flush, Act I
Phone ringing, Act I and Act II
Accordion chords and arpeggios, Act II (if accordion is
    not real)

COSTUME PLOT

Helen Osborne
    Elegant pants suit outfit
    Medium sized heels
    Blouse

James Skipworth
    Worn sport coat
    Jeans
    Sneakers
    White socks

Cuff Link
    Turtle neck shirt
    Slacks
    Tennis shoes

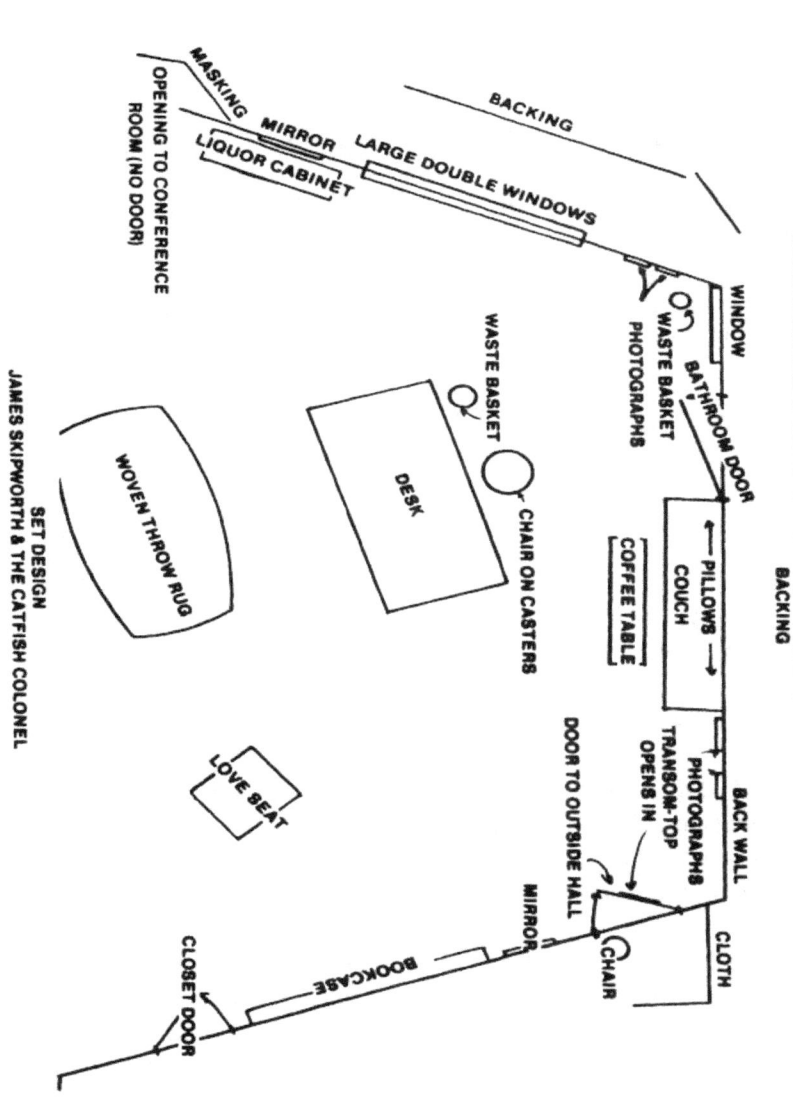

SET DESIGN
JAMES SKIPWORTH & THE CATFISH COLONEL

NOTES AND HOPEFULLY HELPFUL HINTS

SKIPWORTH needs time to build. Become frantic too soon and there's no place to go. Take time in the beginning to firmly establish the two people and their relationship and this will pay off as the pace quickens and finally shifts into high gear with Cuff's entrance.

If SONGS are used for Cuff's "audition." they must be cleared with the proper licensing agencies.

To clarify, Cuff's head is seen through the opaque transom glass each time he jumps up. He may play the scene while standing on a chair and thus let his shadow be seen continuously through the transom, but this takes away from the fun of his popping up and down. At first it may be difficult to get pages through, but with practice it will become easier.

If the actor playing Cuff has other accents and/or voices or even does impressions, these "bits" may be substituted for the written text. The part can be adapted to the actor's special talents.

TELEPHONE: With the old rotary phones, the front mouthpiece can be unscrewed and the round, disc-like speaker element removed. When the mouthpiece is screwed back on, the phone appears normal but the person speaking into the mouthpiece cannot be heard by the other party.

The SET was conceived originally with a large picture window on the back wall above the couch. Helen wrote the letters H - E - L on it with the lipstick and ran out before making the "P," necessitating her making that letter with her body. With an eye to practicality however, the picture window was eliminated and the double windows Right Center were incorporated into the set. It's not as visual to write HELP on the back of the set sketches and stick them in the windows but having a set that's easier to build makes economic sense.

In the initial production the GUN was fired only once, knocking the transom open. However, the more pandemonium that can be created near the end of the play, the more heightened the theatrical effect will be. If exploding liquor bottles and falling posters are in your budget, then let James and Helen fire the gun as many times as possible.

When tying Helen to the CHAIR, James should routine it so this can be accomplished in three or four swift movements with the fifth and final movement being the knot tying. Generally the more practice the actor playing James can put in on mastering this work with the phone cord and the removal of the speaker element, the smoother will be the performance. This is true for all three actors. For Helen, learning to manuever confidently around the set while gagged and tied to the chair will help sharpen her timing. *(A chair with well-oiled casters will be a big help.)*

For CUFF, the routining of his jumps and getting the pages through the narrow opening is essential. Also the actor playing this part must have a strong voice as he has to project through the door from off-stage and often must speak/shout lines while airborne.

The ACCORDION chords can come from the manual playing of the instrument or the sound can be prerecorded and played over the sound system while Helen "fakes" it.

About the Playwright
CY YOUNG

Cy Young has written numerous radio plays for Heartbeat Theater in Los Angeles, animation scripts for Rankin-Bass in New York City, has had three musicals produced Off-Broadway for which he wrote book, music and lyrics, and has a song on the Barbra Streisand Third Album, DRAW ME A CIRCLE. Mr. Young has also worked as a singer/ dancer/ actor in New York and London and performed the title role of James Skipworth in the play's initial production at Riverwest Theatre in the Big Apple.